Pain that felt the size of a large boulder settled in Brian O'Doule's midsection, making it difficult to breathe.

He had failed in his responsibility. He should have seen the ship on the far horizon. That might have given them time to outrun it, especially if they were close to land. As it was now, the pirates gained on them at an alarming rate.

"Angelina." *Tía* Elena shivered. "We must prepare for the worst." Angelina didn't want to think what that would mean. What did pirates do with women?

Tía Elena started praying for protection. "'O my God, I trust in thee: let me not be ashamed, let not mine enemies triumph over me.'"

They were still repeating the words when the door of their cabin splintered open.

LENA NELSON DOOLEY is a full-time freelance author and editor who lives with her husband in Texas. During the twenty years she has been a professional writer, she has been involved as a writer or editor on a variety of projects. She developed a seminar called "Write Right," and she hosts a writing critique group in her home. She has a dramatic ministry, an international speaking ministry that crosses denominational lines, and an international Christian clowning ministry. When she and her husband vacation in Mexico, they enjoy visiting and working with missionary friends. Her Web site is www.LenaNelsonDooley.com.

Books by Lena Nelson Dooley

HEARTSONG PRESENTS
HP54—Home to Her Heart
HP492—The Other Brother
HP584—His Brother's Castoff
HP599—Double Deception
HP615—Gerda's Lawman

Pirate's
Prize

Lena Nelson Dooley

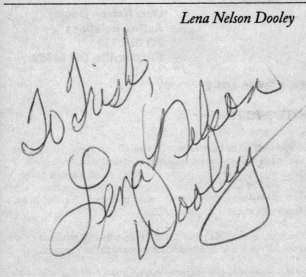

Heartsong Presents

To my brother, Dr. Brian Nelson, a retired pastor, and to my husband's sister, Mary Kelley. James and I love both of you so much.

And, as in all my books, this is dedicated to the most wonderful husband in the world, with whom I have spent more than forty years. James, you have filled my life with joy. Thank you for loving me and taking such good care of me.

A note from the Author:
I love to hear from my readers! You may correspond with me by writing:

Lena Nelson Dooley
Author Relations
PO Box 719
Uhrichsville, OH 44683

ISBN 1-59310-609-2

PIRATE'S PRIZE

Our mission is to publish and distribute inspirational products offering exceptional value and biblical encouragement to the masses.

All of the characters and events in this book are fictitious. Any resemblance to actual persons, living or dead, or to actual events is purely coincidental.

All scripture quotations are taken from the King James Version of the Bible.

PRINTED IN THE U.S.A.

prologue

Late spring, 1805

A closed coach pulled by four black horses bumped over the cobblestone streets of Barcelona, Spain, on its way to the docks. Angelina de la Fuente Delgado clutched the padded seat, trying not to tumble to the floor. She couldn't understand how her *abuela* could remain serenely stationary in the coach. Grandmother sat with her back so straight, Angelina wondered why she didn't bounce off the seat when the vehicle hit a bump.

The musical sound of the Spanish her grandparents spoke filled the air inside the coach. While Angelina was in Spain, she had spoken only Spanish. When she lived in Florida, she had learned English and other languages so she could help her father in the mercantile. The one language she hadn't had a chance to learn was French.

Although it had been over a year since she arrived in Spain to spend time with her grandparents and receive more education, it seemed like only yesterday. This might be the last time Angelina would see her relatives. She reached up and pressed her lips to her grandfather's wrinkled cheek.

"*Nieta.*" *Abuelo* Delgado, who was sitting on Angelina's side of the carriage, took his granddaughter's hand. Angelina turned her attention to him, and he stared intently into her eyes. "We will miss you."

The words sliced through the air and pierced her heart. She knew she reminded him of her mother—the mother she barely remembered. Angelina had been only six years old when her mother died of a terrible fever. She was buried beside the tall palm trees that surrounded the back of their house in St. Augustine, in Spanish Florida. She never had a chance to return to her beloved Spain.

Angelina loved her grandfather's regal bearing. He was a distant cousin of Charles IV, King of Spain. With his snow-white hair and erect posture, he looked like a ruler himself.

Angelina wondered what would happen when she returned to her father. America was so different from Spain, and rules that were rigidly followed in the old country were often ignored in the new. Angelina felt as though she were caught in a strange place suspended somewhere between the two cultures.

She leaned closer to her grandfather's side and whispered, "I will miss you, too." It was hard to get the words past the lump in her throat, and she had to blink to keep tears from spilling down her cheeks.

Abuelo Delgado nodded toward his wife. She opened her *maletín* and pulled a midnight blue velvet pouch from the handbag. The older woman caressed its softness. Finally, Abuela passed the pouch across the coach to her husband.

Doña Elena Vargas Villanueva, Angelina's *duenna* and aunt, watched with as much interest as Angelina did. Until that moment, Tía Elena, her companion and governess, had been looking out the window as if she were disinterested in what went on inside the vehicle.

Abuelo Delgado pulled the drawstring and spread the

bag open, revealing three smaller velvet pouches. He opened the largest one and removed a necklace. "I gave this to your mother on her eighteenth birthday. Since you will turn eighteen next month, I want you to have it."

Seven graduated rubies in an intricate gold setting flashed in the sunlight that poured through the window. Abuelo placed the piece of jewelry in Angelina's lap. She was surprised at how much it weighed. She fingered the links of the chain and watched bloodred fire shoot from the jewels.

Abuelo picked up the second pouch. It contained earrings that matched the necklace. The third bag held a ring. "We want you to have these."

She recognized the jewelry. She had often admired it when she gazed at the portrait of her mother that hung in the *sala* of the house where she and her father lived in St. Augustine. When her parents moved to the New World, the painting was one of the items they took with them.

When the young couple had gone to Spanish Florida to expand the shipping business and establish a *mercantil*, her mother left most of her personal belongings in Spain with her parents. She had planned to return for them. That never happened. Trunks, secured to the roof of the coach and in the luggage boot at the back, held all of her mother's things—all except this jewelry.

Abuela Delgado removed a handkerchief from her *maletín* and dabbed the tears from her eyes. "We will probably never see you again, *mi ángel*."

Angelina carefully put the pieces of jewelry back into the velvet pouches. Then she placed them in her *maletín* before the coach stopped beside her father's ship, bound for Florida.

Angelina took a deep breath. She was sad about leaving

her grandparents, but for some reason, she also felt as if something momentous loomed on her horizon. Something that would change her life forever.

one

Three weeks later

Brian O'Doule hurriedly climbed the rigging of the *Estrella Angelina*—or *Angelina Star*. He loved the feel of the wind blowing through his hair before he reached the crow's nest. He had worked as a sailor on various ships, traveling around much of the known world. By the time he landed in St. Augustine, in Spanish Florida, he had tired of his lack of roots and accepted a job at *Señor* Fuente's company. When his employer asked him to sail to Spain and accompany his daughter and her aunt back home, Brian jumped at the chance to get out of the mercantile and back on the open sea.

Though Brian was not really part of the crew, the captain often allowed him to take a turn as a lookout in the crow's nest. He had the afternoon watch today. The weather had been much colder when they left Spain, but as they moved southwest across the Atlantic Ocean, the air grew warmer. The wind tasted salty and fresh at the same time.

Brian took the telescoping spyglass from his pocket and extended it. He carefully scanned the empty horizon in all four directions. When he pulled the instrument from his eye, his attention moved to the deck below. From way up here, the sailors looked like ants scurrying around the ship.

On the aft deck, an extra sail had been hung on a rope that was strung from post to post like a canvas tent. It sheltered

Angelina and her aunt, when they were out on deck, from the prying eyes of the sailors. Brian noticed a movement on the other side of the sail. He put the spyglass back against his eye and trained it on the deck.

He had a clear view of Angelina and her duenna. That woman kept a close watch on Angelina, and Brian had not been able to get very near her. Angelina. His Angelina. . .he wished.

When Brian had watched the ladies board the ship, he'd been captivated by the beautiful young woman with coal black hair and eyes that sparkled like the sapphires Señor Fuente sold in the store. Long black lashes surrounded those blue eyes. Angelina's lips were as red as the apples that were sometimes for sale in the mercantile. A becoming blush stained her cheeks. *If only. . .* But Brian knew it was no use to dream. He was not the kind of man Señor Fuente would consider allowing his daughter to marry.

Brian enjoyed this opportunity to study Angelina without anyone knowing it. He watched her walk to the railing and turn her face to the wind. Her waist-long hair furled behind her like a flag in the breeze. Occasionally, a few wisps blew into her face, and she reached up with her delicate hand to push them back. The graceful movement sent a pain to his heart. Why was he torturing himself this way?

❧

Angelina had noticed Brian O'Doule as soon as they boarded the ship. She quickly realized that her father had sent him to escort her and her aunt home. Why had he done that? Did *Papá* still think of her as a child? She and *Tía* Elena were women. They did not need a caretaker.

Angelina had been twelve years old when the Irishman

came to work for her father. Back then she had daydreams of a prince coming to the New World and carrying her off to Spain. At first sight, Brian looked just like the prince she had always dreamed about. His wavy black hair curled over the collar of his shirt, and his blue eyes were the same color as hers. They would make a striking couple.

Her dream shattered the first time she heard him speak with that unmistakable Irish brogue. All the Irish people she'd met in the store were fair-skinned with red or blondish red hair. She had never heard of an Irishman with black hair and a dark complexion. He could have passed for a Spaniard if he never spoke.

Angelina rested her back against the rail, using both hands to keep her hair from blowing in her face. The strong wind made her feel free. While they were on the ship, she didn't bother dressing her hair in an elaborate style as she usually did on land. Tía Elena fussed at her, telling her that a lady should always look her best. But that was too much trouble. Besides, the wind would quickly pull it out of its style.

Tía Elena sat on a bench attached to the deck, working on her embroidery. The ship jerked so often, Angelina didn't understand how she could do that without pricking her finger. She studied her aunt intently. Of course, she didn't want to do the handwork herself. She found it boring to sit still and concentrate on something so intricate. Before long, she turned back toward the white-capped waves.

As the water undulated under the influence of the wind, its color constantly changed from a deep greenish gray to a light bluish green, with every shade in between. She would love to find a length of silk that mirrored those colors. What a lovely gown that would make.

Brian slowly scanned the horizon. Nothing but ocean for miles and miles. He tilted the spyglass up and watched a seagull dip and soar in the sky. Perhaps they were nearer to Florida than he realized. He scanned the horizon again, trying to spot the first darkness against the water that would materialize into land as they approached. No matter how long he looked, there was nothing to see.

Finally, he turned the glass back toward the aft deck. Angelina stretched her arms above her head as she leaned on the railing. Her dress pulled tight against her body. Brian shook his head and pulled the spyglass away from the enticing picture. He didn't need to entertain such thoughts. In his first years as a sailor, he'd been friends with the wrong kind of men. He'd done a lot of things—and thought many thoughts—that he was ashamed of now.

When he had settled in St. Augustine, he started attending a church. At first, it was because he had no friends in town. But after the pastor introduced him to Jesus, Brian's life changed.

God had forgiven him. But a man had to be vigilant to keep from stumbling. Temptations were always around, and he didn't want to fall back into his old way of life. Living with Jesus brought pleasures he'd never imagined. The joy of worship and praise. The understanding of how much God loved him—so much that He sent Jesus to die for all those terrible sins he'd committed.

He glanced down once again. Angelina sat beside her companion. She tossed her head, then pushed her abundant curls behind her shoulder. After talking to her friend for a while, Angelina walked back to the railing. She must really like the ocean to spend that much time looking at it. Of course, there wasn't anything else to see out here. That is, unless she would look up at him. He didn't think she even knew who he was. He was just one of her father's employees, and there were many of them.

Brian had no idea how long he spent studying the girl, indulging in daydreams that could never come true, before he heard a dreadful shout.

"Pirates!" First one sailor, then another took up the call.

A cold chill skittered down his spine, paralyzing him for a moment. Brian looked down. The sailors all pointed in the same direction. Brian swung around and saw a ship flying the black pirate flag much too close for comfort. He didn't even need the spyglass to see it. He retracted the instrument with a snap and shoved it into his pocket. Then he scrambled over the side of the crow's nest and descended the rigging like one of the monkeys he had seen in a South American jungle. Once he almost lost his footing in the swaying ropes. It would have served him right if he plunged to his death on the deck below, but he couldn't die now. He had to find a way to protect Angelina and her aunt.

How could he have been such an idiot? Every sailor knew how important it was to continually watch the horizon to keep the ship safe. It didn't matter that there hadn't been anything there for weeks. Nothing should have distracted him from his assignment.

Pain that felt the size of a large boulder settled in his midsection, making it difficult to breathe. He had failed in his responsibility. He should have seen the ship on the far horizon. That might have given them time to outrun it, especially if they were close to land.

The pirates gained on them at an alarming rate. The ship rode high in the water, so Brian knew it must not have as heavy a load as the merchant vessel. Alarm filled him as the sleek schooner sliced through the waves, headed straight toward the *Estrella Angelina*.

ঝ

When the cry of "Pirates" rang out, Angelina and Tía Elena snatched up their belongings and hurried into their tiny cabin. They bolted the door and stood with their backs against it to catch their breath. Angelina's lungs ached with each fearful gasp of air.

"Angelina." Tía Elena shivered. "We must prepare for the worst." She hurried to her trunk and threw open the lid, then pulled a petticoat from it. "Here. Put this on."

After helping Angelina into the garment, she donned a similar one. "There are several special pockets in each of these. Put your jewelry into yours and button the pockets. I will put the money into mine. If we are lucky, we will be able to keep them hidden. If not. . ."

Angelina didn't want to think about what pirates might do with women. She didn't realize she had spoken the question aloud until she heard Tía Elena gasp. The two ladies looked into each other's wild eyes.

Tía Elena started praying for protection. Angelina didn't know anything else to do, so she joined her.

Elena opened her eyes, her expression determined. "We must trust God to protect us. That is the only way we can come out of this alive and unhurt. He is our only hope."

Angelina nodded. A verse played in her thoughts, one that Bridgett Lawson, their cook in Florida, often quoted. " 'O my God, I trust in thee: let me not be ashamed, let not mine enemies triumph over me.'" She quoted the verse, then repeated it. The third time she said it, Tía Elena joined her. Both women continued to chant, "Oh God, I trust in thee. Let not mine enemies triumph over me."

They were still repeating the words when the door of their cabin splintered open.

two

Angelina tried to drown out the sounds of the mayhem outside the cabin by raising her voice in frantic supplication to God. But her words could not overcome the horrendous explosion of heavy wood splintering when the door gave way to the assault. Her body quivered as she whirled to look at the broken portal. A shriek of alarm escaped her lips as her gaze encountered the fierce giant filling the void where the door had been securely latched before he broke it down. Behind him the rumble of battle brought harsh cries and the thunder of clashing metal into the small cabin.

The man stood in the doorway, his gaze raking the space. His eyes widened when he spied Angelina and her aunt. Then an indefinable expression settled on his features, softening them a little. Angelina didn't want to guess what that meant, but at least he didn't look so fierce. She stepped between the man and her frightened aunt, who huddled close to Angelina's back.

"Dear God in heaven." Her aunt's whispered words sounded close to Angelina's ear. "Preserve us in our time of trouble. Protect us from danger."

The man continued to stand with his hands on his hips—a tower of hard muscles covered in black-and-white clothing, dripping with gold chains and medallions, a long sword swinging at his side. The boots on his wide-stanced feet sported jeweled buckles, and hoops hung from both of his ears. The pirate smiled, revealing a glimpse of gold among his stained teeth. Once again, Angelina shuddered, and though it didn't seem possible, her aunt moved even closer to her.

The man's deep voice filled the room with rolling words that reverberated off the close walls. Angelina couldn't understand the words. They sounded French. She wished Brian O'Doule were here with them. She had heard him converse with the French sailors on her father's ships. Although the tone of the pirate's voice didn't sound menacing, the indecipherable words frightened her. He continued to speak, never taking his eyes off Angelina.

"Etienne." A blond young man, who peered from behind the giant, spoke. "What are you going to do with these women?"

At least this man spoke English.

"You aren't going to make them walk the plank with the sailors, are you?"

Angelina wondered what happened when a person walked the plank. She assumed that if they couldn't swim, they would drown. She was glad her father had taught her to swim when she was very small. Then again, that ability might not help her in these circumstances. Where would she go out here in the vast ocean?

The captain glanced at the young man. "No, Walter," he said in English laced with a heavy French accent. "We will take the pretty ladies with us. I will not hurt them. I have plans for the young one."

Everything inside Angelina began to quake, but she tried not to show it. She didn't want the man to know how much his words affected her.

Aunt Elena's hands rested on Angelina's shoulders. "What

did he say?" she asked in Spanish.

Angelina wasn't sure why, but she didn't want the pirate Etienne to know that she could understand him when he spoke English. She answered her aunt in Spanish, the only language the older woman understood. "He says he won't make us walk the plank. He has plans for me." Elena's fingers dug into Angelina's shoulder, but the pain they caused was minor compared to the emotions of abject terror and unbelief boiling within her.

"I have heard about what pirates do to women," Aunt Elena said. "Such things are not spoken about around young, innocent girls." The pointed look Aunt Elena gave Angelina spoke volumes. "Death would be preferable!"

Angelina wondered if she should jump into the ocean when they got out on deck. But something deep inside gave her a sense of peace. Could it be God? After all, they had cried out to Him before the pirate broke down the door.

❧

Brian had raced toward the cabin where Angelina and her aunt had fled. But when the pirates started bombarding the ship with cannon shots, the captain ordered him to help the other sailors control the sails, trying to gain speed.

Too soon, the pirate ship had come alongside the merchant ship and lowered wide gangplanks to connect the two vessels. Brian hid under the makeshift canvas tent that had been constructed for the women. He didn't want to be seen by the men from the pirate ship who swarmed the merchant vessel. Brian didn't carry a weapon, and even if he did, he couldn't protect Angelina. Not that he was in any position to help her during the fray that continued to rage. While he kept out of the way of the swords and cutlasses that sliced through the air, he prayed for Angelina and her aunt. He knew the only way the women could be saved would be by the hand of God.

The pirate captain boarded and ordered his men to drop the anchor to stabilize the ship. The burly man perused the fittings and studied all the items on deck. Then he had his men cross the walkways back to the pirate ship, carrying everything that wasn't nailed to the floor.

The captain of the pirate ship worked his way through the maze and headed for the cabins, almost as if he knew there were extra passengers on board. Brian redoubled his prayers and slipped as close to the stairway as he could get. He knew he couldn't follow without being seen, so he prayed even more fervently.

When he heard the pirates returning, he huddled against the wall and peered around a corner. Angelina and her aunt came through the doorway of their cabin, clutching each other's hands so tightly their knuckles were white. A young pirate followed the women, and the pirate captain strode behind the procession as if he owned this ship. Of course, now he did.

Brian's heart broke when he saw the fear etched on the faces of Angelina and her aunt. He knew he would carry the sight in his heart until the day he died, even if he lived to be a hundred years old. But right now there wasn't much hope for that. These men wouldn't leave anyone alive when they abandoned the *Estrella Angelina*. More than likely, the ship would be scuttled after her merchandise had been plundered.

Oh, God, please show me some way to help Angelina. Don't let the pirates take her away without taking me, too.

❧

Angelina had heard the assault on the *Angelina Star* from

inside her cabin, but she wasn't prepared for the sight that met her eyes when she stepped out on deck. Slashed sail flapped loudly in the wind, and ropes dangled against the blood-spattered deck. Bodies of injured and dead men, who looked like unwanted dolls thrown across the wooden deck in strange positions, lay in growing pools of blood. Clouds of smoke swirled in the air. The acrid odor of spent gunpowder burned Angelina's eyes and nose. She tried not to cough, but she couldn't hold back. She hacked away, doubled over with the effort.

Angelina had never been so frightened in her life. The only thing keeping her from rushing to the side and plunging into the cold water of the Atlantic Ocean was her duenna. She couldn't leave Aunt Elena to the mercy of these men. She would do whatever it took to protect her companion.

A shout of French words spewed from the pirate captain. His men scurried to do his bidding. *Why didn't I learn that language?* The longer she and her aunt shuffled across the deck, trying to avoid slipping on the large spots of blood, the more frightened she became. In her heart, she cried out to God. Bridgett, her father's cook and housekeeper, had talked about the Spirit communicating with God with groanings that cannot be understood. It was the only thing she could do. She didn't know what to say, so her spirit cried out in anguish within her.

Then she spied Brian O'Doule crouched behind a wooden barrel. When their gazes met, she knew he felt the same anguish she did. Some deep communication she didn't understand passed between them, and her fear diminished somewhat.

Once more, French words filled the air, coming from

behind her. Angelina turned to look at the captain. He waited for her to obey his order. She might have if she knew what he said. Aunt Elena cowered beside her, holding on to Angelina's arm as if her life depended on it. And it just might. At least the breeze was blowing away much of the smoke so she could breathe easier.

"Captain." Brian stepped from his hiding place and spoke English to the pirate. "The women do not speak French." He looked at Angelina intently, as if trying to communicate something to her. "They speak only Spanish, so they don't know what you want them to do."

The pirate sauntered toward Brian, his boots sounding a drumbeat against the wooden deck. Angelina prayed silently for Brian's safety.

"What's your name, sailor?" The captain towered over the young man.

"Brian O'Doule at your service, sir."

Angelina almost giggled at the courtly bow Brian gave the captain. She took a deep breath to stop it. Hysterics wouldn't help anything right now.

"I do not want to frighten the women, Mr. O'Doule," the captain said. "Would you tell them that?"

Brian nodded and repeated the captain's words in Spanish.

Hoping Brian had a plan to save them all, Angelina glanced at the captain and gave a slight nod. Speaking in Spanish, she told Brian to ask the pirate what he planned to do with them.

Standing straight and proud in front of the invading captain, Brian repeated Angelina's question in French.

"Tell her I am taking them to my plantation. So we can get to know each other." The pirate smiled at Angelina, again revealing his golden tooth.

It was all Angelina could do to keep from quaking before Brian translated the words for the women. Aunt Elena gasped when she heard what the pirate said. Angelina's stomach heaved, and bile filled her throat.

"I would rather be dead than a pirate's prisoner," Angelina told Brian in Spanish.

"I can't tell him that." Brian spoke her native tongue as well as if he had been born in Spain. "He might kill you."

"And would that be so bad?" After her question, Angelina read the torment in Brian's eyes.

"What is she saying?" The pirate's voice boomed across the deck, interrupting the private conversation.

"She's worried about her aunt." Brian's words contained the truth that Angelina had left unspoken.

"Do you speak French, Mr. O'Doule?"

Brian answered in words Angelina couldn't understand. The rest of the conversation between him and the pirate captain was in French. Angelina wished she knew what they were talking about.

ë

"Yes, I speak French," Brian answered in that language.

"That's good. It's easier for me to understand." The pirate studied Brian's face for a long moment. "Can I trust you, Irishman?"

Brian stared back at the man. "Why would you need to trust me?"

"I must have someone translate for me." The pirate's gaze returned to Angelina. He leered at her like a famished man would look at a banquet table full of food. "My name is Etienne Badeau. I plan to leave the pirating life. I have a plantation where I want to retire, get married, and have a family. This woman would make me a good wife. Do you know her name?"

Brian's heart dropped into the pit of his stomach. Should he go along as a translator and hope for the chance to rescue Angelina before this man could hurt her? Or should he help her try to kill herself? It was a decision no man could make alone. He closed his eyes and cried out to God in his heart. Very quickly, he knew that Angelina wasn't going to die. *Oh, God, if You help me now, I'll make up for my mistake in the crow's nest by rescuing her from her captor.*

"Are you going to help me, Irishman?" The pirate's words brought Brian away from his silent prayers.

"Oui." Brian nodded.

"What's her name?"

Brian didn't want to answer the pirate's question, but he didn't want to make the man angry, either. He would never be able to rescue the women if he didn't play along. "It's Angelina."

The pirate's face lit up at her name. It made Brian's stomach roll. The captain told one of his men to tie Brian's hands behind his back and put him with the two women.

God, help me protect Angelina and her aunt. Please keep me from doing anything that would antagonize Etienne Badeau.

≈

Angelina's heart sank when a pirate tied Brian up. She had hoped he could help her and her aunt escape. Now he was a prisoner, too.

"I'm going with you to translate for you and the pirate." Brian's words didn't make Angelina feel any better. "Don't worry. I believe God will help us escape from these men."

"But there are so many of them and only three of us." Tears pooled in Angelina's eyes. She didn't want the pirates to see them, so she blinked them back.

"I don't know how or when He'll help us, but I do believe that God is on our side."

Brian sounded so strong and certain that for the first time since the initial cry of "Pirates" went up, Angelina had a tiny spark of hope. She looked around the deck at her father's sailors. The ones who were still alive were tied together with a long piece of rope and under the guard of two pirates. The rest of the outlaws moved her father's merchandise from the belly of the *Angelina Star* to the deck of their ship. This attack would cost her father a lot of money. . .and maybe his only child.

The pirate captain indicated that he wanted Brian, Elena, and Angelina to cross one of the large gangplanks to his ship. At first, Angelina didn't think she could do it. When she placed one foot on the undulating board, she glanced down at the churning water below. She quickly looked back at the swaying wooden walkway. How easy it would be to slip off the damp wood. Brian must have sensed what she felt.

"Don't look down." His strong voice gave her strength. "Just look at the ship on the other side and put one foot in front of the other."

After Angelina was across, she turned to watch Aunt Elena, who looked with horror at the board that crossed the chasm between the two ships. A pirate who had been guarding the three of them said something to Aunt Elena, but she remained frozen in place. The man shouted at her, and Brian translated the words.

She tentatively touched one toe to the board. The ship dipped, and she almost toppled over, so she jumped back. The man shouted again, and Elena winced. Angelina wished she was still on the merchant vessel with her aunt.

Brian said something in French to the shouting man. The pirate nodded and untied Brian's hands. Brian touched Aunt Elena on the shoulder. She turned stricken eyes toward him. After speaking softly to her, he put his arm around her waist and helped her up on the end of the board. He stepped up behind her and slowly made his way across the gangplank, holding her tight against the front of his body. Angelina watched a hint of confidence shade her aunt's expression.

When the two of them stepped onto the deck of the pirate schooner, Angelina wished she could throw her arms around Brian and thank him. Instead, she gathered her shaky aunt into her embrace. All three of them stood on the deck of the pirate ship and gazed back at the vessel Angelina's father had named after her.

Four pirates came from behind them. Two of them took hold of Brian's arms and rushed him below deck at the bow of the ship. The other two escorted Angelina and Aunt Elena to the rear of the ship, pushed them up a few steps, and shoved them into a cabin. After the men locked the door, Aunt Elena crumpled to the floor, weeping copiously. For a moment, Angelina felt older than the woman who lay in a heap.

Gazing around the room, Angelina determined this must be the captain's quarters. The cabin spread across the entire width of the ship. A large bunk, hung with what looked like silk draperies, covered the back end. Portholes lined the walls on either side of the room. Angelina walked to one of them and looked at her father's battered ship, still connected to the pirate schooner by wooden planks.

This is a nightmare! But she wasn't going to awaken from this bad dream. Every horrible detail was appallingly real.

Angelina leaned her head against the glass of the porthole and turned her attention to the sunny sky. Through her tears, she watched puffy white clouds scuttle before the wind. A few birds darted around high above the two ships, unaware of the devastation below them. *Please, God, protect us from our enemy. . .and don't let them do anything bad to Brian O'Doule.*

three

Angelina knelt beside her weeping aunt and pulled the woman into her arms. As her chaperone continued to cry, Angelina chanted the scripture that had filled their cabin on the *Angelina Star*. Once again, the words brought comfort to her heart. She hoped they would soothe Aunt Elena, as well.

Nothing that had happened in Angelina's life had prepared her for today. After her beloved mother died, her father had pampered her. Aunt Elena often told him that he spoiled his only child.

Angelina was surprised she hadn't lost control along with her aunt, but something gave her strength. Brian's words about God rescuing them had touched her soul. Bridgett Lawson spoke about God as if He were a man standing beside them. She talked about Jesus as her friend. Angelina grew up in this atmosphere, accepting the existence of God as part of normal life, but she had never felt the need to talk to Him until today. And He had been there for her.

Even though they were still in terrible circumstances, they hadn't been harmed physically. They were probably in the most luxurious accommodations on the ship. Most important, Brian O'Doule was also on the schooner. Brian's words about God rescuing them gave Angelina a fragile sense of peace.

"Where are we?" Aunt Elena seemed to have cried herself out. She sat up and looked around, swiping tears from her cheeks with both hands. "Is this the captain's cabin?"

Angelina stood and helped her aunt to her feet. "I believe it is."

Her duenna began wringing her hands. "Do you think this is a good thing? What if he wants to have his way with you?"

Although she wasn't exactly sure what those words meant, Angelina didn't want to think about it. "Brian O'Doule said God will rescue us. I believe him."

Aunt Elena stared at Angelina. "How can you be so sure?"

"I don't know." Angelina held out her hands. Earlier she couldn't hold them still, but now they were steady. "I should be falling apart, but Brian's words brought comfort and strength to my heart."

The older woman wandered around the room. When she started toward one of the portholes, Angelina said, "You don't want to see what's going on out there."

"Yes, I do." The words were firm. Perhaps her companion was stronger than she appeared.

❧

The pirates threw Brian into a tiny, dark cell. The only light came through the bars on a window that was cut in the heavy door. At least it wasn't completely black, and the cell was close enough to the open companionway that he had fresh air. But he didn't care about his own circumstances; he worried about the women. Where had the sailors taken them? He hoped the captain had sense enough to put them in his own cabin. And he hoped that if Badeau had put them there, he wouldn't share the room with them.

Brian's heart still contained the assurance from God that He would rescue them, but his mind kept reviewing all the terrible things that could come about before that happened. Brian was glad that years ago Pastor Harold Blodgett had convinced him to memorize scriptures. Many verses he learned comforted him during the long hours he spent not knowing what was going on above deck.

Brian spoke the words from Psalm 56 aloud. " 'What time I am afraid, I will trust in thee. In God I will praise his word, in God I have put my trust; I will not fear what flesh can do unto me.' " A blanket of comfort covered his heart, so he repeated the verse over and over. Each time he said it, he felt a deeper presence of God surround him. If only he could know what was happening with the women.

Father, I don't fear what the pirates can do to me, but I'm afraid for Angelina and her aunt. Please, God, protect Angelina from any evil thing Etienne Badeau might plan to do to her. I know I deserve to be a prisoner. If it hadn't been for my inattention, the pirates might not have been able to overtake us. Help me find a way to escape and rescue the women. That's the only way I can redeem myself. Make me alert to everything around me so I can discern Your direction when it comes.

After his prayer, Brian tried to figure out what was going on outside his dungeon. Although he could hear the murmur of voices, they were so far away he couldn't tell what was being said. The rumbling, scraping sound of barrels and crates being shoved across the deck punctuated the indecipherable conversations. Soon the pirates would probably start transferring items into the hold.

The brig was near the outside hull of the ship, so Brian also heard waves lapping against the wood, sounding like a soft drumbeat. He could imagine the cries of the gulls that dipped and floated above the havoc. Once again, he wondered just how far they were from Spanish Florida.

In the darkness, loneliness closed in around Brian, almost suffocating him with its intensity. He started speaking his thoughts out loud to banish the feeling, but he didn't want any of the pirates to know what he was saying, so he whispered in Spanish.

"If I try to escape with both women at the same time, our progress will be slow and we'll probably be recaptured." His voice brought a little life to the darkened cell. "That pirate would then execute me, leaving the women at his mercy. . .or lack of it. I could travel more quickly alone. I could run for help to rescue the women and to capture the outlaws. These men need to be stopped, and they must pay for the crimes they've committed."

But where could he get assistance? If he escaped from the ship near shore, whom could he trust? Any port the pirates might approach would undoubtedly be in a raw, undeveloped land filled with lawless men.

If he could return to Señor Fuente, Brian was sure the man would give him the aid he needed. But first, Brian would have to confess his own part in allowing the attack. His boss might never forgive him. Still, if he wanted to rescue the women and capture the pirates, Brian would have to convince Angelina's father to trust him. *God, I need Your help*.

ɐ

Aunt Elena stood at the porthole transfixed by what she saw, a look of horror on her face. Angelina moved toward the next porthole so she could see what was going on.

Elena turned toward Angelina. "Mi ángel, it might be best if you didn't watch. I am supposed to be protecting you, and I have been remiss. Please, come away from the porthole."

"I have to know what's happening." Angelina pressed her

nose against the cold glass.

The enormous captain strode across the deck as if searching for anything the other pirates might have left behind. He spoke to one of his men, but from this distance, Angelina had no idea what he said. The sailor started toward the cabin where Angelina and her companion had stayed during the voyage. When the man came back on deck, he was carrying one of Angelina's trunks. He took it to the captain.

Etienne Badeau, upon seeing the trunk, barked out orders to two other pirates, who hurried toward the cabin. They returned carrying Angelina's other trunk and Aunt Elena's. Angelina hoped they weren't going to throw the baggage overboard.

As two pirates carried the women's trunks across the gangplanks to the pirate schooner, Etienne Badeau returned to their cabin. When he came back on deck, he was carrying their hand luggage. Angelina shuddered to think of that awful man touching her personal items.

The pirate captain strode across one of the gangplanks as if it were level ground.

Aunt Elena turned from her porthole. "What do you think that man is going to do with our things?"

Angelina glanced at her and shrugged. "I don't know."

A knock sounded on the door of the cabin.

"Who—?" Angelina cleared her throat, trying to dislodge the lump that impeded her words. "Who's there?"

French words sounded through the wooden door. Angelina shivered. She stepped to her aunt and grasped her hand.

"Walter," the pirate said in English, "go get the Irishman. I need him to translate."

Angelina let out the breath she hadn't realized she was

holding. "He's getting Brian," she explained to her aunt.

Aunt Elena wrung her hands. Angelina quoted the scripture they had used before. " 'O my God, I trust in thee: let me not be ashamed, let not mine enemies triumph over me.' "

❧

Brian stopped talking to himself when he heard footsteps approach his cell door. As the key scraped in the lock, he got up from where he had been sitting on the floor.

The blond Englishman stepped through the doorway. Walter something, if Brian recalled correctly.

"Mr. O'Doule, the captain requires your services." The man approached with a length of rope in his hands.

"Walter, if I promise not to try anything, would you leave me unbound?" Brian knew it was a long shot, but he had to try. "It'll upset the women to see me tied up."

The man looked deep into Brian's eyes before he nodded. "All right. But try anything, Irishman, and you'll die."

For an instant, fear sliced through Brian, but the words from Psalm 56 played in his head again. Did God prompt the words this time?

Brian followed Walter across the deck and up the steps to where Etienne Badeau waited outside a cabin door. From its position on the ship, Brian surmised it led to the captain's quarters. Perhaps the pirate was respecting the women's privacy, after all. The thought made him breathe a sigh of relief.

"Irishman." The pirate spoke in French. "I need your help."

The captain thrust a large skeleton key into the lock on the door and turned it. Brian wondered if the screech of metal against metal scared the women.

When the door opened, Brian saw Angelina and her aunt

standing together with their heads held high as if they were unafraid. He could tell that fear lurked behind their forced expressions, but he hoped Etienne Badeau didn't recognize it. Brian was proud of the women's bravado. He tried to convey his feelings to Angelina with his gaze.

"Irishman," Badeau said, "tell the women they'll be safe in this cabin on the voyage."

When Brian translated the message in Spanish, both women looked relieved.

"Tell them I've brought all their luggage from the other ship."

Angelina nodded after Brian repeated the message.

The pirate captain went out into the passageway and bellowed in French. Several of his men appeared, carrying trunks. They deposited them against one wall of the cabin. Badeau went outside for a moment and came back in, holding the hand luggage.

"Tell them I am sorry I had to touch their belongings, but I did not want any of my men to do it."

Angelina's eyes flashed when Brian conveyed the message. His heart broke for all the assaults on her sensibilities. *Oh, God, I'm so sorry I brought this on her.*

❧

Too soon, the pirate escorted Brian from the cabin, shutting and locking the door behind them. Angelina slumped, tired from holding her body erect. Her aunt rushed to the porthole and peered out. Angelina's attention was also drawn toward what was happening outside.

With her holds empty, the *Angelina Star* rode high in the water. She had been a beautiful ship before the attack, and Angelina had been proud she bore her name.

Aunt Elena turned her attention toward her ward. "What do you think they will do with your father's sailors?"

"I don't know." Angelina hoped he would spare them, but she knew that hope was probably in vain.

She turned back to the porthole. Etienne Badeau strode across one of the gangplanks and stood before the prisoners. He spoke to them, then waited. Two of the men nodded. The pirates untied them from the rest of her father's sailors. Other pirates escorted the two across a gangplank to the schooner. Angelina had heard about sailors who agreed to join the pirates rather than face death. But she had never expected any of her father's men to do so.

She knew that whatever came next would be gruesome, but she had to watch. The captain spoke again, and one of his men slid a small plank through a slit in the side of the merchant ship. The prisoners were untied from one another. Using short lengths of rope, the pirates tied each sailor's hands behind his back. One by one, they were led to the plank and forced to walk to the end, then jump.

Angelina let out a gasp. Her father's sailors were going to their deaths. She knew that few of them could swim. Besides, it would be almost impossible to stay afloat with their hands tied. That beast was killing them as surely as if he had thrust his saber through their hearts. How could he treat her and Aunt Elena so well and kill the others?

And what about the men who had come aboard the pirate ship? Had Etienne Badeau offered them a place on his crew? If so, would they be prisoners for a while, until he felt he could trust them? Her head buzzed with the questions that whirled in her brain.

After the last sailor left the end of the plank, all the

pirates returned to their schooner. Before the captain left the merchant ship, he grabbed the rope holding the anchor. With a quick slash of a knife he pulled from a sheath at his waist, he cut the anchor loose.

After he returned to the pirate ship, his men pulled the large gangplanks back aboard their boat. Once again, the cannons began firing at the *Angelina Star*.

Each time a ball hit the hull, Angelina felt as if she herself were being battered. Over and over, the wood splintered. The pirates aimed the balls at the vessel's waterline, and water rushed through the holes. Her father's favorite ship sank deeper and deeper into the ocean. After a few minutes, one end tipped lower than the other, going completely under the surface of the water. After a moment's hesitation, the rest of the *Angelina Star* slipped beneath the surface of the Atlantic Ocean. When she disappeared from sight, Angelina released the sobs that tore at her heart.

four

As the pirate schooner pulled away from the sunken merchant ship, Angelina couldn't tear her gaze from the area where the *Angelina Star* had slipped beneath the waves. She felt as if that spot was her only connection to her father. But as they sailed farther away from the field of debris and bodies, she felt that tie loosen. The hope that she would see her beloved parent again diminished as the distance grew. Her heart cried for the warmth of his arms cuddling her to his chest, his strong, soothing voice reassuring her that everything would be all right. He had been her anchor in every storm since her mother died. She felt that nothing would ever be right again.

When the debris became tiny smudges on the rippling surface of the ocean, Angelina finally turned away from the porthole. She looked around their luxurious prison cell, finding nothing familiar except the luggage against one wall.

Aunt Elena made her way across the swaying room and sat on the curved lid of her trunk. "Come, child, sit down." She gestured toward one of Angelina's trunks. "It is not very comfortable, but I do not want to touch anything that belongs to that awful man."

Angelina rubbed her arms as she paced across the expanse of empty floor. "I thought Papá said that piracy was no longer a problem on the high seas."

"It was much stronger in the mid-1700s, before the majority of the pirates were captured or killed. Most people feel perfectly safe traveling on the oceans now." Elena leaned over and picked up her reticule, then worked to untie the handbag's drawstring. "But a few pirates continue to ply their trade. Unfortunately for us, this French giant is one of them." After she finished looking through the contents of her bag, she clutched it to her chest. "It doesn't look as if anyone bothered my belongings."

Angelina picked up her own handbag and peered inside. "Mine, either." She glanced around the unfamiliar room and shook her head. "I wonder how long we will remain safe here."

Her duenna dropped her bag on the floor beside her trunk. She stood and pulled Angelina into her arms. "We will stay strong and face whatever comes. I will try not to show my weakness again."

The two women clutched each other for a moment. Then a loud knock on the door resounded through the room.

❧

Brian rapped on the wooden planks covering the entrance to the captain's quarters, hoping he hadn't startled the women. He waited for a moment but heard nothing. Fearing that something had happened to Angelina, he motioned for Walter to unlock the cabin.

When the portal swung back, the room appeared empty. But when the door opened wide, he saw Angelina and her aunt close to their trunks by the wall, almost behind the door. Although they stood ramrod straight, he noticed a fragility about them that hadn't been there before. Of course, after all the devastation that had occurred that day, even the strongest woman would be affected. As would any decent man, himself included. But he needed to remain strong for the women.

"Walter brought me to have supper with you."

Brian heard the door close behind him. The rasp of the key in the rusty lock punctuated his sentence.

Angelina rushed across the room. "I am so glad to see you." She threw her arms around him. Surprised, he stood still, enjoying the embrace.

"Mi ángel," Elena cautioned, "do not throw yourself at the man. Whatever will he think?"

Brian looked across Angelina's shoulders at her aunt. "It's all right." He enclosed Angelina in his arms, trying to comfort her. "She's been through a lot today."

After patting her on the back for a moment, he turned her around and walked beside her toward her duenna. "I've been praying for both of you."

Angelina turned concerned eyes toward him. "Where are they keeping you?"

"Below deck." Brian didn't want her to know about the dark, smelly cell.

"In the brig?" Her eyes dared him to try to keep from answering her.

He couldn't do it. "Yes. . .but it's not. . .so bad." His words sounded hollow, even to his own ears.

Angelina gave him an empathic look. "I have seen the brigs on many of my father's ships. They are nothing but dark holes."

Brian stared into her eyes. "It's not the best of accommodations, but at least I'm on the same ship with you. I'll do all I can to keep you safe. . .somehow."

The scrape of the key in the lock interrupted their conversation. Walter entered carrying a tray with three bowls on it. The aroma of well-seasoned beef filled the cabin.

"Here now," Walter said in English. "This is your stew. I'll go back for the bread and water." He set the bowls on the table, then turned toward Brian. "Aren't you going to tell them what I said?"

Brian realized his error. He had almost given away the fact that Angelina could speak English. He nodded, then turned to the women and repeated in Spanish what the young Englishman had said. He was going to have to stay alert. One more mistake like that could cost one or all of them their lives.

❧

The stew consisted of fresh meat and vegetables. It had been awhile since Angelina had tasted anything so savory. And the biscuits were far better than the hardtack they had been eating the last couple of weeks on the *Angelina Star*. She had been longing for the tasty fare they enjoyed at the beginning of their journey. The first few bites of her food began to satisfy the emptiness in her stomach. Having Brian share the meal with them added to her enjoyment.

Their time together was interrupted by the scratching of the key in the lock. Angelina looked at the doorway. The French giant filled the opening. He smiled at the group gathered around the table and swept his hat from his head with a courtly bow. Was he trying to impress them? She had to hold herself erect to keep from fainting.

His words were unintelligible until Brian translated them. "Etienne Badeau says that he will join us for supper."

As soon as Brian finished speaking, the pirate moved an empty chair to the table and sat in it. Walter followed him in, carrying his food. After he served his master, the cabin boy left the room.

The delicious food turned to sawdust in Angelina's mouth. It took the rest of her mug of water to wash down the bite she had been chewing. Etienne Badeau spoke to Brian, and Brian translated the words in Spanish; but Angelina wasn't interested in what the pirate had to say. Her eyes roved the room to keep from looking at the captain. She moved her spoon around in the wooden bowl, playing with the chunks of meat and vegetables that swam in the rich brown broth.

Brian's words sank into her awareness when he announced that Etienne Badeau wanted to take all his meals with them. Angelina almost gagged. She stopped even trying to pretend she was eating.

Once again, Brian spoke to the pirate, and comprehension dawned on the man's face.

"What did you say to him?" Angelina whispered to Brian.

"I told him it might not be a good idea for him to eat with you just yet because you've just suffered a great shock."

Angelina glanced at the pirate's face. A look of sympathy lit his eyes. The man was a paradox. With a quick shout, he summoned his cabin boy.

After Walter removed the captain's food, Etienne Badeau stood and addressed them. When he finished, he strode through the door before Walter locked it behind him.

"What did he say?" Aunt Elena asked.

"He doesn't want to add to your distress." Brian smiled at Aunt Elena, then at Angelina. "He won't force his presence on you. He'll give you time to get used to the idea of being on his ship."

Angelina heaved a sigh of relief, but she couldn't take another bite of her food. "I'm glad."

"That's not all he said." Brian rose from his chair and stuffed his hands in the front pockets of his trousers. "He'll be coming back soon to remove his personal effects from this cabin. He won't use it for the remainder of the journey. But he's going to let me come here for meals. He's hoping that will help you feel more comfortable."

Angelina looked up at Brian. "That may take quite awhile. I want to keep you out of the brig as much as we can."

ॐ

Brian was glad Angelina cared about his comfort, but he knew he would need to be careful in front of the pirate. If Badeau guessed that Brian had feelings for Angelina, the man wouldn't hesitate to get rid of him. He silently asked God to help him be all he needed to be until he could rescue the women.

Badeau left them alone for over an hour, obviously not wanting to interfere with the women's mealtime. But Angelina just played with her food. Brian didn't see her take even one more bite, and Elena only nibbled on her biscuit.

With their bowls still half full, the women returned to sitting on their trunks. They looked very uncomfortable perched on the curved tops.

Brian stayed in his chair at the table. "I'll watch carefully for a way to escape from the pirates."

Angelina's eyes grew as big as saucers.

"But I won't put you in danger. I want all of us to escape from his clutches. I just don't know how long that'll take." Brian took another bite of the stew. He, too, had lost his appetite, but he knew he needed to keep up his strength, so he finished the serving.

From across the room, he saw tears sparkling on Angelina's dark lashes. It made him want to go to her, take her in his arms to shelter her, and assure her that everything would be all right. But although he still felt that God was with them and they would be okay, he couldn't lie to her. Everything might not be all right, at least for a while.

❧

Even after the captain removed all his belongings from the cabin, Angelina still didn't feel comfortable there. When Badeau left, he took Brian with him.

Angelina scanned the room, feeling the pirate's presence in every corner. But she and Aunt Elena couldn't just huddle on their trunks. They had no idea how long the voyage would be. When Brian came back, she would ask him where this plantation was that the pirate had mentioned. Maybe then she would know more about what to expect.

Aunt Elena stood. "Well, it looks as if we're going to be here awhile. We might as well make ourselves at home." She brushed her hands down the front of her skirt, pressing out the wrinkles. "After all, we can't sleep on top of our trunks."

The image of them trying to sleep on their luggage brought a smile to Angelina's face. "I suppose you're right." She crossed to the bed that was built into the back wall of the cabin. "This is large enough for both of us to sleep comfortably, and there are clean linens here."

Angelina made the bed, then started to change clothes for the night. When her dress dropped to the floor, she noticed the petticoat Aunt Elena had given her. She had become so used to the weight that was evenly distributed around her body, she'd forgotten all about it. She looked down at the lumps made by the jewelry in the hidden pockets of the undergarment. When she glanced up, she saw her aunt watching her.

Elena untied the drawstring holding her petticoat around her waist. "Let's hide these in the bottom of our trunks. I think they will be safe there. The captain seems to respect our property."

❧

Angelina hadn't expected to sleep well, but when she awakened at dawn, she couldn't remember a thing since stretching out on the soft mattress. She didn't even have bad dreams, which was a wonder after all she had observed the day before. She slipped out of bed and made her way to the portholes on the opposite side of the ship. She didn't know if she could ever look out the one where she had watched the destruction of her father's ship and crew.

Sunrise painted pastel colors across the few clouds that rode in the sky—pinks, lavenders, and pale yellow against the robin-egg blue background. She knew that soon the colors would turn intense, but the early dawn made the world outside the ship seem new and fresh. When a sliver of the rising sun peeked over the horizon, it sent a trail of sparkling jewels among the gentle waves. How could the world look as if nothing was wrong? Yet tranquility spread before her. Were they near land? Angelina couldn't see any on this side of the ship. Dare she look on the other side? Before she could decide, Aunt Elena stirred, causing the bedclothes to rustle. Angelina turned and looked at her.

"What do you think will happen today?" Her aunt stretched to get the kinks out of her back.

"I don't know." Angelina went to her trunk and pulled out a dressing gown. "It will be hard, but we'll have to trust God. He has taken care of us so far."

Aunt Elena padded barefoot across the room to her own

trunk. "I think we should dress soon. We don't know when the captain will return."

"I only hope he brings Brian O'Doule with him."

a

Brian had just risen from his pallet when the door to his cell opened.

Walter stood in the opening. "Etienne told me to take you to have breakfast with the women."

Brian frowned. "Is he going to be there, too?"

Walter shrugged. "I don't think so."

Brian smiled. "I'll be glad to eat with them again."

After reaching the companionway, Brian took deep breaths of fresh air as they traversed the wooden planks to the poop deck. When they arrived at the cabin where the women were, Brian knocked.

"Why do you do that?" Walter asked as he turned the key in the lock.

"If we just unlock the door and go in, it might upset the women. I don't want to scare them." Brian went through the door, and Walter locked it behind him.

Angelina stood silhouetted against the light that streamed through the portholes. His heart skipped a beat. She looked breathtaking with the golden rim of sunlight on her raven curls. She must have awakened early, because she was fully dressed and every hair was in place. Too bad he would never be able to tell her how he felt about her. On this ship, it would be dangerous, and if they ever escaped, her father would have a hard time forgiving him for the danger he had put her through.

"Good morning, Brian." Her melodious voice wrapped around his heart, holding it captive.

"Angelina." He nodded at her. "Did you get any rest?"

She walked toward him. "Yes. Thank you for asking."

Brian turned toward Elena. He was afraid that if he didn't, he would give himself away. "*Y usted, señora?*"

The older woman smiled at him. "I slept surprisingly well."

The key scraping in the lock signaled Walter's return. The young man brought in their breakfast, placed it on the table, and left without a word.

Elena took a bite of a hot biscuit, then turned toward Brian. "Did you sleep well, Señor O'Doule?"

"Oh, you don't have to worry about me, señora."

"But you probably do not even have a bed, do you?" A look of distress dropped over Angelina's face like a veil.

"I've slept in many places that weren't any more comfortable than where I am on this ship. I'm all right." Brian smiled at each woman in turn.

"What do you think of Walter?" Elena said, changing the subject. "He seems a bit old for a cabin boy. He must be in his twenties."

Brian laughed. "I don't think pirates run their ships the same way merchants do. I'm sure the captain needs someone he can trust in charge of his cabin. Walter seems to be loyal to Badeau. I'm not sure everyone on the crew is, though."

Angelina looked up from her food. "Why do you say that?"

"Even below deck, I hear a lot of what's going on." Brian laid his spoon beside the bowl of porridge. "The captain moved into the first mate's cabin and made him bunk with the rest of the crew. From what I hear, the first mate is pretty angry about that. Badeau may have a problem if he's not careful."

Angelina placed her hands in her lap. "Do you know where his plantation is?"

Brian took a bite of his biscuit to delay answering her question. The captain hadn't told him anything about the plantation. It could be anywhere—on an island in the Caribbean Sea or somewhere in the Atlantic Ocean or even in some wild, unsettled land farther west. He didn't think they were headed east or south, so it probably wasn't in the Atlantic, but it could be anywhere else. He'd heard that many ports, such as New Orleans, were havens for unlawful men. Brian hoped they weren't going that far west.

"I'll ask him if I see him again," Brian said after swallowing his food.

His answer brought a glimmer of hope into Angelina's eyes.

❧

The next day, Brian asked Badeau Angelina's question, but he didn't receive an answer. Evidently, the pirate captain didn't want them to know too much.

A couple of days passed before Brian was able to figure out a little about the direction the ship was going. The best he could tell, they had gone in a southwesterly direction. Now they had turned almost due west. If he had it right, they were going around the south end of Florida. He knew the plantation probably wouldn't be in a very populated place. He prayed fervently for an opportunity to get the women away from the Frenchman before it was too late.

The best part of the voyage was the time he spent with the women while they were eating. After a few days, however, he realized they were growing pale and listless.

"Señora Elena," Brian asked over their midday meal one day, "is there anything the two of you need?"

The older woman looked at him. "Although this room is spacious for a ship's cabin, it is a very small space. We feel as if we are in prison. We need to be out in the sunshine, but we don't want to be around the pirates."

"Aunt Elena is right." Angelina put down her fork and leaned toward Brian. "At least on my father's ship, we were able to spend some time on deck."

"I understand." Brian agreed with the women, and he wanted to do all he could to help Angelina and her aunt. But Badeau was unpredictable. If Brian asked and he refused, the women would be disappointed. He didn't want to add to their burdens. He would see what he could do. If the pirate did agree, Brian would be able to give them a pleasant surprise.

ဆ

Angelina paced across the floor. They had been on this ship for several days, and she had no idea where they were or where they were headed. "I think I'm going to lose my mind."

Aunt Elena looked up from her needlework. "I know, mi ángel. If I didn't have something to do, I would feel that way, too. Why don't you try some needlework? I have more that I can share with you."

Angelina shook her head. "You know how hopeless I am at things like that."

Her aunt put her handiwork in a basket by her feet. "There is a bookshelf on that wall. Is there anything on it you want to read? It might take your mind off our plight."

"I haven't wanted to touch those books because they belong to that man." Angelina walked over to the shelf and read the spines. "But there are some interesting volumes here."

Before she could reach for one, a key scratched in the lock. Angelina stepped back to stand beside where her aunt was sitting.

When Angelina saw Brian in the doorway, she couldn't

keep from smiling. His presence made their horrible situation more pleasant.

The French giant had not bothered them since that first day. So she was surprised to see him enter the cabin behind Brian. Angelina quickly turned her attention to the man in front.

"Etienne Badeau asked me to tell you that he has made arrangements for you to go out on deck at least once every day." Brian smiled at the women. "I will accompany you."

The Frenchman's voice filled the room. Although Angelina had always liked the cadence of the language, it was hard to keep from shuddering at the sound.

"He wants you to be comfortable," Brian translated.

Angelina felt like telling the pirate that if he wanted them to be comfortable, he shouldn't have attacked her father's ship.

Once again, French words rolled around her.

Brian cleared his throat. "He wants to know if there's anything else you need."

To be set free. . .To never have to see the man's face again. . .To see my father. . .To have the last few days never have happened. Angelina could think of many things she needed, and none of them included the awful pirate who smiled at her with a gleam in his eyes—and from his gold tooth.

five

Brian glanced up at Angelina from his seat on an overturned wooden bucket. She looked so beautiful with the wind kissing her cheeks, giving them a rosy color, and with the blue sky as a background.

She stood with her back to the railing, her forearms extended along the top. Her hands held the protective barrier so tightly, her knuckles turned white. "Do you think my father knows his ship has been destroyed?"

"I don't know." He ran his hand through his hair, pushing the too-long curls out of his eyes. If they ever got out of this dilemma, he would look for a barber to trim his hair and to get rid of this beard that made his face itch. "He might just think we've run into bad weather that slowed us down. . .unless someone comes across the debris." His words weren't comforting, but it was the best he could do right now.

Angelina sighed. "I don't want him to think I've been killed."

He might think you've been kidnapped. Brian didn't want to give Angelina more to worry about, so he refrained from voicing that thought.

The winds had been capricious that day. Early in the morning, they blew at almost gale strength, skimming the schooner across the waves at a fast clip. But now the air was still. Brian noticed the sails shifting, trying to harness any breath of wind. The captain knew what he was doing, but all his efforts were in vain. The ship moved only slightly. The surface of the ocean was almost as smooth as a looking glass, with the few fluffy clouds overhead reflecting in it. He hoped this calm wouldn't put Badeau in a bad mood. On more than one occasion, Brian had heard the man bellow at the sailors. He hoped the women hadn't noticed. When the pirate captain was angry, he reminded Brian of a lion he'd heard roaring the one time he visited Africa. The sound brought fear to the hearts of every man who heard it.

Angelina sat beside her aunt, then turned toward Brian. "Do you have any idea where we are?"

He had tried to sidestep that question in the past, but after scratching his beard a moment, he answered her as honestly as he could. "I'm pretty sure we're heading west. . .or northwest across the Gulf of Mexico."

"Where will that take us?"

Brian rested his arms on his thighs and clasped his hands between his knees. "I don't know for sure what Badeau has in mind. But I think we might be heading for New Orleans."

Angelina's eyes widened. "Isn't that in the wilderness?"

Brian straightened, then stood. "If we go farther west, we'll be in Mexican territory. And that might be worse than New Orleans."

The women shivered at his words.

"Angelina," Brian said, "tell me why you went to Spain." He knew the answer, but if he could get her to talk about pleasant things, maybe he could rid her mind of the dark thoughts that brought deep shadows to her eyes.

While they talked, heavy clouds scudded across the horizon and piled up in the sky not far behind them. When thunder rumbled and lightning split the clouds, Walter took the women to the cabin so the men could return to the deck.

The sails billowed and flapped in the driving wind. Though the ship moved faster, they couldn't outrun the storm. The pirates brought down the sails to keep the ship from capsizing. Soon after, torrents of rain battered the vessel. As soon as he could take a quick break from his work, Walter took Brian back to his cell.

Down in the brig, Brian felt the waves pound the hull as it bobbed up and down on the crests and troughs of the angry sea. With nothing to hold on to in this dark hole, he was tossed from wall to wall. Finally, he snagged the bars in the door. Gripping with all his might, he leaned his head against the cold metal, pulling as close to the wood as possible to anchor his body.

"Father God, please protect the women. Calm their fears." Brian's heart ached within his chest, knowing how frightening it was to be on a ship in a severe storm. These strong winds could be part of a hurricane. If so, this ship might be doomed. He continued to cry out to God from the bottom of his heart.

❧

Angelina had never been on a ship in a storm this bad. Everything in the captain's cabin was anchored to the floor, but the heavy trunks containing their personal effects slid partway across the floor with each movement of the vessel. Almost unable to stay on her feet, Angelina looked around the room, trying to find a safe place.

Aunt Elena clambered into the bed. "Mi ángel," she called above the fury of the storm, "come here."

After Angelina slid onto the mattress, her companion raised the railing and struggled to lock it into place. Angelina hadn't noticed the railing before, thinking the wooden bars to be just a decoration on the side of the bed.

"We should be safe here." Aunt Elena pulled Angelina into her arms and leaned against the wall.

The two women rolled from one side of the bed to the other. Water lapped against the portholes, often covering the glass completely for minutes at a time. Were they going to die here on this ship?

"O my God, I trust in thee: let me not be ashamed, let not mine enemies triumph over me." Aunt Elena repeated the words Angelina had taught her during the pirate attack.

How could Angelina forget that God had watched over them so far? He had protected them from harm by the pirates, and He could save them from this storm. But how much more would they have to endure before He finally rescued them?

The women grabbed rungs in the railing to keep from being thrown against the walls. Angelina hoped the latches wouldn't pull out of the planks. She lost track of time while the storm battered the ship. Several times she thought the wind might break it into a million pieces.

❧

When the storm finally abated, Brian's arms felt sore, almost as if they'd been pulled from their sockets. His shoulders ached, and his body was battered and bruised. He would be sore for several days from the beating he'd endured from the storm. He wondered how the women had fared.

"It's time to take down the Jolly Roger."

The words, spoken by a sailor outside his cell, startled Brian. Why were they taking down the flag with the skull and crossbones? Was that how Badeau hid his identity when he was in port? Were they close to land? Brian wished his dark room had a porthole so he could look outside.

When Walter came to get Brian for the midday meal with the women, Brian was able to see where they were as they crossed the ship's deck. Not far in front of the ship, he saw a large gulf filled with muddy brown water.

"What river is that?" Brian asked Walter.

"The Mississippi."

Brian studied the thick forest that lined the banks. The underbrush could hide anything—wild animals, marauders, other pirates. He'd heard about how wide the mouth of the Mississippi was but had never seen the amazing thing with this own eyes. "Have you been here many times before?"

"We come here all the time," Walter said. "Badeau's plantation is upriver a ways from New Orleans."

They reached the door to the cabin, and Brian knocked before Walter inserted the key in the lock. "Will Badeau stop in New Orleans this time?"

When Walter pulled the door open, the hinges screeched in protest. "I doubt it. He won't want anyone to know about the women. New Orleans is a raw, rough city. At least along the river, it is."

As soon as Walter left the room, Brian rushed to the portholes to see what he could from the sides of the ship.

"Come and eat, Brian," Elena said. The woman seemed to worry about him as much as she did her niece.

He turned around to face the women. "We've entered the mouth of the Mississippi River. I want to see all I can before Walter takes me below."

Angelina left her bowl of stew and came to stand near him. She looked out the porthole beside his. "It's a long way to the bank."

"Yes. The Mississippi is the widest river I've heard about.
Brian crossed the cabin and looked out a porthole on the other
side. "We're about in the center of the river. It's as far to thi
bank as it is to the one on the other side." He turned back
and faced the women. "I'm hoping there are some settlement
along here. We might need help with our escape."

Elena glanced up from her meal and turned a piercing gaze
toward him. "Are you so sure we'll escape, Brian O'Doule?"

He smiled at the older woman. "Yes, I am. God has protected
us this far. He won't stop now."

She returned his smile before starting to eat again.

Brian had only taken a few bites of his stew when
Walter returned to take him back to the brig. While the
two men walked across the deck, Brian etched as much o
the surroundings into his memory as he could. He would
contemplate what each thing meant while he was in his cell.

❧

After Brian left, Angelina paced from one side of the ship
to the other, studying the banks of the river through the
portholes. Sometimes the schooner shared the water with
small fishing boats, but they were scattered far apart.

The pirate ship had been sailing up the river for two or three
hours when Walter brought Brian back to the captain's cabin.
Angelina was glad to see him again so soon. Unfortunately,
Etienne Badeau followed the other two men into the room.
Angelina's welcoming smile turned to a frown when she saw
the pirate.

The giant man's voice boomed. Brian translated the words
into Spanish. "Mr. Badeau says we are approaching New
Orleans. It's important that no one knows you're on the ship.
Will you women agree to stay away from the portholes until

he tells you it's all right?"

Angelina didn't want to agree. She wanted to scratch the pirate's eyes out, if only she could reach them. "What will he do if we don't agree?"

Brian grimaced. "Probably lock you somewhere without portholes."

His expression begged her to agree. It occurred to her that he was talking about a cell such as the one where he was being held.

"All right." She heaved a sigh. "We'll stay away from the portholes."

Brian relayed her answer to the pirate. Badeau's eyes bored into her as if to gauge whether she was telling the truth. Finally, he gave a curt nod, then exited the cabin with Walter.

Brian came to Angelina and took her hands. "You did the right thing. We shouldn't give Badeau any reason to doubt us. There is no way to escape right now anyway."

Angelina studied Brian's face. "Are we going to New Orleans?"

He released her hands and stepped back. "No. Walter told me the plantation is upriver from there. I don't know how far."

Elena put down her needlework and stood. "Do you think it is in the wilderness?"

"My guess is that it is." Brian rubbed his forehead with his thumb and forefinger. Angelina wondered if he had a headache. "I can't imagine him being anywhere near where other people live."

&

Brian's prediction proved to be right. Even from his cell in the belly of the ship, he could tell when they sailed past New Orleans because he heard carousing. On through the evening hours and most of the night, the ship slid through the muddy river water at a slow speed.

Well before dawn, Brian heard the crew members moving around on deck. He felt the ship list to the right. He expected the movement to stop soon, but the river must have made a sharp turn or they had slipped into a tributary.

About dawn, Walter came to take Brian to eat with the women. When the two men stepped up on deck, Brian saw that the ship was anchored in a hidden cove. Huge trees with long, thin branches that brushed the ground surrounded the ship. Some kind of gray substance hung from most of the branches, giving the trees a ghostly aura. Bobbing in the water near the shoreline were several small boats with oars.

Brian leaned over the rail and looked at the water, which no longer looked as muddy. "Are we still on the Mississippi?"

"No. The river's down that way." Walter jerked his hand back over his shoulder. "We came up a bayou to get to this cove." He hurried toward the cabin door.

"What's that gray stuff on the trees?"

"Spanish moss." Walter waited for Brian to knock before he inserted the key in the lock. "Kind of spooky, ain't it?"

🙠

When Brian arrived for breakfast, Angelina turned from looking out the porthole and watched Walter carry in the tray with their food.

"They'll take us to the plantation house as soon as we finish eating." Brian dipped a spoonful of porridge.

Angelina put her spoon back into her bowl. "How far is it from here?"

"I'm not sure."

After they finished their meal, Walter led Brian and the

two women out on deck, where a dinghy was tied to the side of the ship. One of the sailors sat in the back, manning the oars. Walter had Brian descend the rope ladder first. Then he helped Angelina over the side to start her descent. Brian guided her to the bottom of the small boat. When Angelina turned around, Aunt Elena started down the ladder.

Walter joined them, barking orders to the rower in the back. The sailor headed toward a slight opening between some low-hanging branches. The boat parted the curtains of Spanish moss and headed through a wide bayou.

Clinging to both sides of the boat, Angelina marveled at all they passed. Tall trees near the waterline held hanging gray fronds. Sunlight filtered through the limbs high above, casting an otherworldly glow on the shadows. Strange sounds surrounded them, echoing in the lofty branches. Insects swarmed around them, and Angelina and her aunt had to let go of one side of the boat to swat them away.

No one spoke, as if a word would break the spell surrounding them. A shiver started deep inside Angelina. She didn't like the feel of this place. A log on the bank suddenly sprouted legs and walked toward the water. A low roar bounced across the water. Aunt Elena screamed and covered her face with her hands. Brian's eyes widened.

"You might want to keep your hands inside the boat." Walter's voice penetrated Angelina's thoughts. "Them gators might take a bite." Brian repeated the words in Spanish.

Although she pulled her hands close to her chest, Angelina was mesmerized by the animal skimming just below the surface with two bulging, unblinking eyes sticking out of the water.

"If you don't make any sudden movements or loud noises,

it might just swim on by."

Aunt Elena looked as if she were going to faint. Brian took the duenna's hand to steady her. Angelina smiled her thanks to him.

When they rounded a bend in the waterway, Angelina could make out a two-story house in the distance. It sat on a rise above the water, surrounded by a large lawn.

When the sailor pulled the boat up to a dock, Walter stepped out on the wooden planks. "Brian O'Doule, if you promise not to give me any trouble, I'll not tie you up."

Brian nodded, then stepped out of the boat. The two men helped Angelina and Aunt Elena from the dinghy.

The four of them followed a path up the open hillside between two areas of moss-swaddled oak trees. When they neared the end of the walkway, Angelina was surprised to see that the two-story house was practically a mansion. What a surprise to find such an impressive place in this godforsaken swamp.

A broad veranda spread across the front of the house, with a balcony the same width decorating the second story. Wide steps led up to the veranda. On either side of the steps, windows at ground level revealed the presence of a basement. At both ends of the structure, new walls had been put up, indicating that additional rooms were being added. The holes where the windows would go looked like vacant eyes.

As they walked up the steps that led to the portico, Angelina wondered if she and her aunt would be locked in the basement.

Walter opened the carved door and led the way into a foyer with a marble floor. The massive room was two stories tall, and curving staircases wrapped around each side of it.

Before Angelina could take in all the amenities of the room, Walter started up the stairs. When the women didn't follow, he turned back.

"Your rooms are up here." He waited for them to cross the foyer before he continued up the stairs.

As they walked down the wide hallway, Angelina silently counted the doors they passed. "Are these all bedrooms?"

After Brian translated her question, Walter nodded. Then he unlocked the last door on the left and stepped back so the women could enter.

Such luxury! The house where she and her father lived was nice but it was nothing like this. The sun pouring through the windows on the far wall streamed across the hardwood floor, reflecting in its bright shine. Several paintings in ornate frames hung on the whitewashed walls. Although the room contained several pieces of furniture, they were arranged in pleasing settings and the area didn't seem at all crowded. Its open feel would have been welcoming under different circumstances.

"Come with me," Walter ordered Brian as he left the room. "You're going to help us get the booty out of the ship."

Angelina didn't want Brian to leave. She felt less uncomfortable in this strange place with him there.

He hesitated just outside the door, looking back at her. With her gaze, she tried to communicate to him how much she wanted him to stay.

Walter pulled Brian out of the room, then locked the door on the women.

Angelina hurried across the room and stepped out on the balcony, where she watched the two men return to the dinghy. A breeze teased her hair, bringing welcome coolness from the smothering humidity of the swamp that surrounded the house and grounds.

They were still prisoners of Etienne Badeau, even if their cell was more luxurious than any prison she had ever heard of. *God, what is going to happen to us here?* Angelina felt a jumble of emotions whirl around inside her. After spending a year in Spain, all she wanted to do was go home to her father. Instead, she had become the prisoner of a horrible pirate. Everything in her world was out of control. She wanted to trust God, but it wasn't easy. How much more could she take? When would this nightmare end?

six

After watching Brian and Walter make their way down the long walkway to the boat dock, Angelina stepped back inside her suite of rooms in Badeau's mansion. Aunt Elena stood in the middle of the sitting room, taking in the luxurious accommodations. Angelina's heels sounded a quick staccato as she walked across the polished inlaid wooden floor to join her aunt.

"These are lovely." Angelina walked over to two settees that faced each other across a low table on one side of the large room.

Aunt Elena dropped onto one of the couches. "They're comfortable, too."

On the other side of the room, two high-back chairs upholstered in fabric with a woven design of roses on a dark green background sat on each side of a smaller table. The flowers on the chairs were the same shade as the claret-colored fabric that covered the settees. A large oil lamp with a white shade rested on the table. It would be the perfect place to sit and read or write letters.

A mirthless laugh burst from Angelina. She knew the pirate wouldn't let them write letters to their family. If her father had found out about the ship sinking, he would have assumed they all were dead. When that thought entered her mind, tears slipped down her cheeks.

Oh, Papá, I miss you so much.

Aunt Elena got up from the sofa and skirted around the table in front of it. She walked to the door in one wall. When she tried the knob, it turned. "I wonder what's in here."

Angelina hurried across the room to join her. The door opened into a large bedroom. The tallest four-poster bed she had ever seen sat against the opposite wall. It was so high off the floor they would need a step stool to get into it. A beautiful quilt covered the lofty mattress, and fluffy pillows leaned against the carved headboard. Angelina went over to test their softness. She wondered where the pirates had stolen these from. No woman would want to part with something she had lovingly pieced together, probably from scraps of the clothing her family had worn. If she weren't so tired, Angelina would be tempted to request another room. Then she remembered that everything in this house had probably been stolen from someone.

Angelina found a stool pushed partially under the edge of the cover. She pulled it out and climbed up. When she lay on her back across the bed, her weary body sank into what had to be a feather mattress. After all the time on the two ships with their hard berths, sleeping in this bed would be heavenly.

A rocking chair with a needlepoint cushion on it sat near the washstand in each bedroom. Colorful flowers were painted on the pitcher and matching bowl. The dressing rooms off the bedrooms contained a large wardrobe with hanging space and drawers made of cedar. If Angelina unpacked everything in both her trunks, it wouldn't have filled the space in her dressing room. She didn't know anyone who owned enough clothing to fill both this wardrobe and the chest of drawers that sat across the room from the bed.

"Do you suppose we are to share this bedroom?" Aunt Elena walked over to the carved chest that had a large cheval glass above it. The frame of the mirror allowed it to tilt so they could see themselves from head to toe.

"I don't know. There was another door on the opposite side of the parlor."

Both women hurried toward it. Angelina turned the knob. They entered a space that was a twin to the other bedroom.

Angelina put her arm around her aunt's shoulders and gave her a squeeze. "We each have a bedroom of our own." She walked to the windows overlooking the front lawn. "And both bedrooms have a door to the balcony."

Aunt Elena trailed her fingers along the tall footboard of the massive bed. "This suite is larger than many houses." She clasped her hands close to her chest. "But it is still a prison, isn't it?"

Angelina nodded as tears once again slid down her cheeks. She reached up and swiped them away with the backs of her hands. In other circumstances, she would enjoy visiting a house like this, but not now. Not like this. How long would they have to be in this place, and how would they ever get back home?

❧

When Walter and Brian arrived at the schooner, Badeau put them to work helping the pirates unload the holds. The *Estrella Angelina* had not been the only ship the pirates had robbed on this voyage. Badeau assigned three crew members to each of the four small boats. After loading the dinghy with all the booty it could safely haul, two pirates and a rower made the trip up the bayou. When they reached the dock near the house, the pirates carried the load up the hill, and the rower waited for their return.

On their first trip to the house, Walter walked in front of Brian. Each man carried a well-used sea chest on his shoulders. The edge of the wood dug into Brian's back, so he knew the chest he carried was full. The cabin boy led the way around to the back. Set at an angle in the ground, an open wooden door rested on an earthen mound, leading down a flight of steps to the basement.

As they descended the concrete stairs, Brian admired the large chiseled rocks that formed the outside wall on both sides of the stairwell. The stairs were steep, but the opening was wide enough for the men to get their burdens through the doorway.

The sun streamed through the portal, painting a large irregular rectangle across the first room in the basement. Sturdy rock partitions divided the underground area into several rooms. Walter opened the door to one that was situated under the center of the house. The structure was partially filled with an abundance of merchandise, undoubtedly from other pirating forays.

"We'll put these things against this wall." Walter carefully set down the wooden box he carried and slid it into place along the wall. "Etienne likes to keep the booty from each voyage separated from the others. I think he tallies the take from each ship."

Brian placed the box he carried next to Walter's. It felt good to have the heavy weight off his shoulders. He stretched trying to get the kink out of the middle of his back.

As they headed toward the stairs to the outside, Brian's gaze darted around the shadowy basement. The windows didn't give much light, but he couldn't see any other way out of the area except the door where they'd entered. All the windows were near the ceiling, and they were too small for a man his size to squeeze through, even if he could reach one of them.

When he and Walter emerged from the basement, they met two more pirates carrying wooden crates on their shoulders. The men frowned at Brian. When he was in the brig on the schooner, he had heard some of the pirates complaining about his being allowed to eat with the women. Obviously they didn't think he was being treated like a prisoner.

Moving all the merchandise and treasures from the ship to the plantation house took several hours. Before they finished, Brian was glad he had built up his strength with the good food on the pirate ship. He wouldn't have lasted otherwise.

After he and Walter made their last trip up the hill, the Englishman led Brian to one of the other rooms in the basement. Vertical iron bars on the small window in the door proclaimed its use. Another cell. How was he ever going to escape from Badeau's men and rescue the women?

Walter opened the door, and Brian glanced around the room. A tiny window near the ceiling let in a little light. At least the place had a bed with a thin mattress, making this prison better than the brig on the ship.

"It's not much." Walter grimaced and rubbed the back of his neck. "If you don't try anything, Badeau will learn he can trust you. Then maybe he'll move a lamp and a few other things in here to make it more comfortable."

Was this going to be Brian's future? Hidden in a tiny cell in a basement? At least he was too tired to care that night. Even the narrow bed looked inviting.

❧

Three of the pirates brought the women's trunks into the

suite and placed them in the dressing areas off each bedroom. After they left, Angelina and her aunt took out only enough clothing to last them for a week. She hoped, by then, Brian would figure out how to rescue them.

Elena came through her bedroom door. "Angelina," she said in a hushed voice. "Are you wearing the petticoat with the jewels?"

She nodded. "Do you still have the money in yours?"

"Yes, mi ángel." Her companion led the way into the dressing room. "I think we should hide the petticoats in the bottom of our chests again."

She helped Angelina fold her petticoat with the jewels tucked inside it, then placed it in one of the chests. Together, they repacked all of Angelina's extra clothing on top. Then they went into Aunt Elena's dressing room and did the same thing with the petticoat containing the money.

After they returned to the sitting room, Angelina heard a knock on the main door to the suite but didn't hear a key in the lock. "Who's there?" she asked.

Brian's voice came from outside the room. "Walter would like to bring our supper up here."

Angelina opened the door and smiled at Brian. Though fatigue painted his face, he smiled back. She had seen how many trips he had made up the hill from the bayou with burdens on his back. She wanted to reach up and smooth the lines on his forehead but knew she shouldn't. "Are you alone?"

"No." He nodded toward one end of the hall. "Walter is waiting for an answer."

Angelina stepped into the hallway enough to peek around the door and see the Englishman standing at the top of the stairs. "*Gracias*," she said to Brian. He smiled. "Please tell him we would like to eat now so we can get to bed soon. Aunt Elena and I are very tired."

Brian turned and relayed the message in English to Walter. Then he stepped through the open doorway. "This looks comfortable," he said, studying the suite.

The door closed, and the key turned in the lock, reminding Angelina once again that she was a pirate's prisoner.

"It's really quite nice." Angelina led the way to one of the closed doors. "We each have our own bedroom." She opened the door so he could see.

Brian glanced inside. "Badeau is building quite a house here, isn't he?"

Angelina sat in one of the chairs in the parlor. Elena had handwork spread around her on one of the settees, so Brian took the other chair.

"I don't know how long we'll have to be here." Brian frowned. "Everything is under heavy guard. At least you'll be comfortable. . .if Badeau doesn't do anything to harm you."

"Do you think he will?" Angelina shuddered. The man was a vicious pirate, no matter how well he had treated them. "He hasn't done anything bad to us yet."

Brian's eyebrows drew together in a troubled frown. "I'm sorry. I didn't mean to frighten you. You're right. I don't think he will bother you."

Angelina looked at her hands in her lap and noticed numerous wrinkles in her skirt. After all they'd been through, she must look an awful mess. Wanting to look her best for Brian, she rubbed at her skirt, trying to flatten out the wrinkles. It was little use.

"Do you know where you will be sleeping?" she asked.

Brian didn't want to upset Angelina. He knew she wouldn't be happy about his new cell. "Downstairs."

"Are there bedrooms on the lower floor?"

Brian scratched his beard, trying to think of a way to make his accommodations sound better. "There are some rooms in the basement." At least that wasn't a lie.

Angelina stared at him a moment as if trying to read his expression. "What kind of rooms?"

He propped his foot on his knee. "All the pirate booty is stored in one of the basement rooms. Food is stored in others. The cook came down and got some supplies while we were unloading the ship. I'm staying in. . .another room."

Angelina stood and placed her hands on her hips. "Are you in a cell?"

Brian sighed. She certainly was a stubborn woman. But he liked that. "Badeau doesn't trust me, so of course he'll lock me up. It's a cell, but not as bad as the brig on the schooner."

She crossed her arms over her stomach. "How is it better?"

"There's a window, so I have sunlight. And I'll be able to sleep on a bed instead of the floor."

Elena gasped. Brian saw a look of sadness cover the woman's face before she looked away.

Tears glistened in Angelina's eyes. "Oh, Brian, we are in so much trouble."

He stood and gathered her into his arms, and she sobbed quietly. Brian was glad to comfort her, although he would have preferred to hold her when he didn't need a bath so badly.

seven

Arturo de la Fuente couldn't help worrying about the *Estrella Angelina*. According to his calculations, the ship should have arrived in Spanish Florida by now. Even if there was a lot of stormy weather when they crossed the Atlantic Ocean, it shouldn't have been delayed this long. Every time a ship came into port, he inquired if they had sighted his merchant vessel. But he always received a negative answer. He worried about the merchandise he needed to restock the store, but more than that, he anguished about his beloved daughter. His life would have no meaning without her. Ever since his wife's death, Angelina was all he lived for. Why had he let her go to Spain to visit her grandparents? At the time, it sounded like a good idea, but if anything happened to her, he would never forgive himself.

His right-hand man, Brian O'Doule, was also on his flagship. The Irish sailor was like a son to him. Arturo pinched the bridge of his nose. A headache pounded between his eyes. He turned back to the open ledger in front of him. The figures were beginning to run together. He closed the large book and slid it on the top shelf under the counter.

The bell above the door jingled. Arturo looked up to see who was coming into his establishment. The tall stranger with graying hair walked with the rolling gait of a man who spent his life on the ocean. He had the commanding presence of a sea captain, but instead of sailing clothes, he wore a fashionable suit.

The man came straight toward the main counter, not even glancing at any of the merchandise.

"How may I help you?" Arturo moved around the end of the polished wooden counter and approached the newcomer.

"Are you Mr. Fuente?" A frown wrinkled the stranger's brow.

"Yes."

"My name is Roger Cabot. I wonder if I could take you to supper after the store closes."

The man's troubled expression indicated that he carried a heavy load on his soul. People often arrived in town without knowing anyone, and Arturo always tried to make anyone who came into the store feel welcome.

"Would you like to eat at my home? My housekeeper is the best cook in St. Augustine. And she always prepares enough food for several people, even when there's just the two of us at a meal."

Mr. Cabot fingered the lapels on his suit. "I wouldn't want to impose."

"I'd be honored to share my evening meal with you." Arturo held out his right hand. "Besides, if you don't help me eat it, Bridgett will have to make up a food basket and find someone else who needs the food."

With a grave smile, the man took the proffered hand and shook it. "I would be honored to be a guest in your home. Where do you live, and what time should I arrive?"

Arturo returned the man's smile. "Actually, it is about time to close the store. Since there aren't any other customers, I'll lock up now." He started toward the front. "I own the house behind the store."

After he secured the door and pulled the shades on the front windows, Arturo led Mr. Cabot through the storeroom to the back door. They walked across the walled flower garden that separated the two buildings. A profusion of colorful blossoms draped along the retaining wall and clustered beside the door to the adobe dwelling. The flowers made Arturo think of Angelina, and for a moment, worry for her flooded his mind.

When Arturo opened the door to his house, enticing fragrances of roasting meat and hot bread met them. The two men made their way through the salon to the dining room.

"Bridgett, please set another place. We have a guest." Arturo gestured for Mr. Cabot to sit in the chair beside his own.

Bridgett bustled into the room carrying an extra plate and glass. After she put them in front of the visitor, she hurried to the kitchen and returned with a white napkin and silverware.

"Sure and I'm glad that Mr. Fuente has someone to share his meal." She gave Mr. Cabot a broad smile before she left to fetch the food.

As they consumed their supper, the two men discovered a lot about each other. The stranger was indeed the captain of a whaling ship. He was from New England in the United States. Arturo told him how he had come from Spain to Florida and established his business. He even mentioned his beloved wife, who was buried in the garden, and the fact that his daughter had gone to Spain to visit his wife's parents.

"What is a whaling captain doing so far south, Mr. Cabot?"

Arturo wiped his mouth with the linen napkin and scooted his chair back from the table. "I thought men like you spent most of your shore time farther north."

Roger cleared his throat. "I hate to bring bad news at the end of such a good meal, but I think I have something that belongs to you."

Arturo leaned forward. "What could you possibly have of mine?"

Mr. Cabot stared off into the distance. "As my ship was coming back to port with a full hold of whale oil and blubber, we happened across a field of debris in the Atlantic several nautical miles east of here. Bits and pieces of wood were scattered here and there. The farther north we went, the more debris we encountered. Finally, we found a couple of bodies."

A sharp pain lanced Arturo's heart. He didn't like to hear about anyone being lost at sea, and the thought introduced a new fear. What if the *Estrella Angelina* were also lost?

"We pulled them aboard and then gave them a decent burial at sea. Then we came across the thing that has led me to seek you out."

Arturo swallowed the lump of fear that was growing in his throat. "What was it?"

"A piece of wood with the words *Estrella Angelina* painted on it."

Arturo clutched his hands in his lap to keep from grabbing his chest.

"We needed to get back to our home port as quickly as we could, so we kept sailing. After arriving in Boston, I took care of our load, paid my crew, and greeted my family. Then I set out to find the owner of the *Estrella Angelina*. That search led me here. It was your ship, wasn't it?"

A sob clogged Arturo's throat. "Was one of the bodies you found. . .a woman?"

"No."

The man's whispered words pierced Arturo's heart. "My. . .only daughter. . .was on that ship."

eight

In the week since their arrival at the plantation house, Brian came every day to eat with Angelina and her aunt. For the evening meal, Etienne Badeau also joined them. Angelina enjoyed breakfast and dinner when the pirate wasn't there. Even though he was the perfect gentleman every time he came, supper with him was always uncomfortable.

Angelina didn't have to wonder what the pirate captain did with the rest of his time. Most days, sounds of hammering resounded through the clearing near the house, and she often stood on the balcony watching the pirates working on the additional rooms. Even though she couldn't often see Badeau from her vantage point, she heard his thundering voice shouting orders to the men who worked on the building.

She especially looked forward to the noonday repast, when Walter left Brian with them longer than at the other two meals. They discussed their childhoods, and Angelina felt as if she knew him well. For a man who traveled the world with rough sailors, Brian showed a certain refinement.

Besides the time when they were eating, the women spent the rest of their day sitting in the suite of rooms or on the balcony outside.

For most of the day, the balcony was shaded, so Angelina spent quite a bit of time out there. She needed to breathe the fresh air after the close confinement on the pirate ship. Of course, the air here felt heavy with moisture, and during the middle of the day, it was too hot to be out, even in the shade.

Angelina wiped the perspiration from her brow with her handkerchief and got up from the low chair on the balcony. She parted the sheer silk curtains and entered the parlor. "Isn't it about time for dinner?"

Aunt Elena glanced up from her embroidery just as a knock sounded on the door. "I believe you're right." She folded the edges of the pillow cover she was working on and placed it in the basket beside her feet. She patted a few errant curls back into place as if she wanted to look her best for Brian.

Angelina crossed the room and opened the door. "Is that fresh bread I smell?"

Brian followed Walter into the room. Each man carried a tray.

"Yes."

"We must be near the kitchen, because I can smell everything that's cooking. It makes me ravenous by the time the food is served."

Brian repeated what they said in English for Walter.

In this house, Walter had become a different person. Instead of a junior role, as he had on the schooner, he was in charge of running the household. He carried all the keys, and Angelina often observed him giving orders to some of the other pirates who worked in the mansion.

Walter set the food on the table by the settees and backed out of the room, locking the door.

Just after he exited, a loud boom echoed through the house, causing Angelina and her aunt to jump.

"I wonder what that was." Angelina put her hand on her chest, trying to still the frantic beating of her heart.

"I don't know." Brian sat on the settee opposite from the one where the women sat. "We can ask Walter when he returns."

Brian lifted a bowl toward his face and took a sniff. "What do you suppose this soup is made from? It doesn't smell like chicken or beef."

Angelina dropped onto the settee beside Aunt Elena. "I don't care what it is. It smells good, and I'm hungry."

She grabbed a thick slice of warm brown bread, already slathered with butter, and took a bite. The rich flavor melted in her mouth. She took a spoonful of the soup. "You're right. This doesn't taste like anything I've ever had before. I hope it isn't one of those awful alligators."

Brian looked up from his food. "Walter told me to ask if you needed anything."

"We need to launder our clothing," Aunt Elena said before Angelina could answer.

"One of the sailors takes care of the washing for the men." Brian took a bite of the bread. "Maybe he could do yours, too."

Elena's eyes widened, and she pulled one hand close to her throat. "We don't want a sailor handling our unmentionables."

Brian put his food down. For a moment, a flush of red covered his cheeks. "Of course. I'm sorry. I didn't think."

Elena reached over and patted his hand. "Don't worry about it."

"I'll ask Walter if something can be done."

"Thank you." Elena picked up her glass of water and took a sip.

"Brian." Angelina looked into his bright blue eyes. "What do you do all day? I hope they don't keep you locked in that cell all the time."

Brian stood and ambled over to gaze out the open door of the balcony. "I'm let out of the basement whenever Badeau has a job for me. He has me take food to the men working on the house. I occasionally help with the yard or the laundry. I've even helped with the construction, even though I have never had experience as a carpenter. Sometimes I feel like a slave, but at least I get out in the sunshine for a while."

Angelina wished she hadn't asked.

When Walter returned to collect the empty dishes and take Brian back to his cell, Brian asked, "What kind of soup did we have today?"

"Turtle."

It was all Angelina could do to keep from reacting to what the man said. She couldn't let him know she understood his words. But how could anyone eat turtles? They lived in dirt and slime. Of course, eating a turtle might be better than eating one of those horrible giant lizards that lived in the swamp around them.

Brian turned toward the women. "Walter says it's turtle soup."

His smile at Angelina's gasp told her he guessed what she was thinking.

She glanced toward Walter. "I have another question. Please ask him what that loud noise was that we heard earlier."

Brian translated as he helped Walter gather the dishes onto the tray.

Walter stared at him a minute, then shrugged. "I guess it wouldn't hurt to tell you. The two men from your ship who joined Badeau's crew got tired of working on the house. They told the captain they wouldn't do it anymore."

"What happened to them?" Brian asked, following the

Englishman to the door.

Walter's answer drifted back into the room before he closed and locked the door. "Badeau shot them."

Angelina grabbed Aunt Elena and clung to her. Brian hadn't translated the Englishman's words, but Angelina understood every one.

"What's the matter, mi ángel?" Her companion patted her back to soothe her.

Angelina debated whether to tell her aunt. She didn't want to upset the woman further. But she thought it important that her aunt know the truth about their barbaric captor. "Badeau shot the two traitors from my father's crew."

Aunt Elena's face went white, and she clutched Angelina tighter. "God rest their souls."

How could the pirate captain be so nice to them and so ruthless with other people? Only a monster could kill people in cold blood. She would have a harder time than ever not revealing her contempt for him the next time he came into her room. But what would he do if she couldn't hide her disgust?

※

Brian paced across his cell floor. After two weeks, his plight wasn't any better than it was when they arrived at the plantation. At least Badeau provided clean clothes for Brian to wear when they ate. And Walter had let the women out of their rooms long enough to do their laundry. He even allowed Brian to watch over them, to protect the women from the pirates. Of course, a guard stood close by to make sure they didn't try to escape.

When the pirates came to get him to help with the construction on the house, he labored as hard as anyone, more than some. Badeau worked along with his men, but he didn't hear the grumbling that Brian did. Some of the men didn't want to be carpenters; they only wanted to be sailors. Brian was surprised that some of them hadn't left. Maybe they were waiting for Badeau to divide the booty with them.

Brian's thoughts turned to Angelina. When they ate with Badeau, it was hard to hide from the pirate how much he cared for her. Because of the heat, she had taken to putting her hair up. Curls often sprang loose from their confines and formed a halo around her sweet face. Since she spent so much time out on the balcony, her cheeks had been kissed by the sun, adding a golden glow to her creamy complexion.

He knew better than to entertain longings for what could never be. Why couldn't he have been born in Spain? Then her father might consider letting them marry. A Spanish father would want his daughter married to a fellow Spaniard. If Brian were able to escape and rescue her, her father might forgive him for causing this travesty. But he would never agree to a marriage. Brian didn't have the same social standing as Angelina and her father. Besides, Señor Fuente was a strong Catholic, and Brian attended the Protestant church in St. Augustine. Señor Fuente wouldn't want his daughter marrying outside his church.

When the key scraped in his door, Brian stopped his pacing and faced Walter. "Is it time for supper?"

Walter set a bucket of fresh water on the floor. "You have about fifteen minutes to clean up." He handed Brian fresh clothes.

After he had washed and dressed, Brian put on the clothes. They fit as if they had been tailored for him. He wished he had a looking glass. Walter had stayed long enough for him to shave one day last week, but Brian knew his cheeks sported a beard that was several shades lighter than his dark curls. Would he ever again have the chance to shave every day?

♣

Angelina hadn't felt this good in more than three weeks. Walter had delivered a copper bathtub in the middle of the afternoon. After having several of the men bring up buckets of water to fill it, he left without saying a word to the women. Angelina offered to let Aunt Elena use the tub first, but she declined. Now Angelina's hair and body were squeaky clean. She put on her lightest summer dress, then pulled back her still-damp hair and tied it with a ribbon that matched the warm pink of the garment. It was one of the latest fashions when she left Spain. The scooped neckline and the white lace trimming the empire waist made her feel feminine. For the first time since they arrived in this place, she liked the way she looked. If only Brian would notice.

When Brian and Badeau arrived for the evening meal, Angelina waited for them, seated on one of the couches. Aunt Elena sat beside her so the pirate wouldn't.

Brian and Badeau sat on the opposite settee while Walter and another of the pirates brought in the food. Angelina noticed that Brian looked especially handsome tonight, even though his beard had grown back. She was sure that many women probably flirted with him. Thankfully, he was a godly man who didn't believe in trifling with a woman's emotions.

Badeau launched into his usual evening banter. Angelina didn't really listen to his words anymore. She simply waited for Brian's translation.

"Is there anything you need that you don't have right now?" the captain asked through Brian.

How could she answer a question like that? *I want to go home to my father. I want Brian to look at me and really see me.* Angelina felt a blush creep into her cheeks. She hoped no one would notice.

"Badeau says he's going to stop his piracy. He wants to be a legitimate plantation owner." When Brian looked her in the eyes, Angelina let her gaze drop to where her hands rested in her lap. "He plans to marry and have a family."

Why would the pirate captain tell her all this? It had nothing to do with her.

"I want you to be happy, Angelina." The pirate's words coming from Brian's mouth went straight to her heart. They sounded as if Brian meant them himself.

Angelina glanced up at him. For an instant, the expression on his face seemed to echo the words. Then, as if a veil were drawn over his countenance, his expression was masked.

Before Angelina could think of anything to say, the pirate continued. This time Brian's words sounded more impersonal. "Badeau wants to take you through the house and get your opinion on what else needs to be done."

Suddenly, it hit her. On the ship, Badeau said he had plans for her. The pirate spent every evening meal with her trying to get to know her. Why had it taken her this long to understand? He hoped to marry her. She turned toward Brian. Surely he didn't go along with this idea.

Badeau said something else. Brian looked at her. "Angelina, I'm not going to tell you what he just said. But you must act as if you are going along with him."

The idea of taking a stroll through the house with this abhorrent man made her skin crawl.

"I know you don't want to do this, but it might be the only way we can eventually escape. Let him take you through the house. I'll be with you. Act as if you are comfortable here. I have a plan."

Angelina bowed her head and took a deep breath. She could sense Aunt Elena's agitation, but she would do what she had to. Brian had a plan, and she would trust him. She raised her head and gave a tremulous smile to no one in particular.

◆

As Badeau gave Angelina and her aunt the grand tour of the massive house, Brian followed the trio. He asked for Angelina's ideas on everything, and she answered in clipped monotones. Every time Badeau tried to move closer to her, she stepped back. Brian saw her hands shake before she clasped them together to make them stop. He noticed tension in her shoulders and neck. She obviously abhorred the man and hated spending any time with him.

By the time the tour was over, Angelina's shoulders were sagging, and she picked nervously at her fingernails. Brian's heart hurt to see her this way. Even being locked in his cell in the basement didn't cause him as much misery as watching Angelina suffer.

During the midday meal, which they ate without the pirate's oppressive presence, Angelina told Brian how much she hated being around Badeau. And when the captain joined them for supper, she was silent and aloof, refusing to respond to any of the man's comments or questions.

After they finished eating their food, the frowning pirate

stormed out of the room. Brian had to step lively to keep up with the man.

"Badeau," Brian said, taking two quick steps to the pirate's one, "I've not given you any trouble, have I?"

The pirate stopped short and peered down at him. "What are you talking about?"

"I've cooperated with you completely." Brian lifted his chin defiantly. "I've translated for you, worked for you, and done everything you asked me to."

Badeau placed his hands on his hips. "So what if you have?"

"I want to be treated better."

"But you're my prisoner." Badeau sounded amazed that Brian had the audacity to say what he did. "You eat well. I give you new clothes. What else do you want?"

Brian took a deep breath. "I want some more things to make my room in the basement comfortable. A better mattress. A chair. A lamp so I can see at night. Maybe some books to read."

The pirate glared at him. "And why should I do all this?"

"So I will continue to translate for you."

The giant glowered at him. "I could have you killed instead."

Brian stood his ground. "Yes, you could. However, I am a man of honor, and I will cooperate with you in every way." Brian knew he wasn't being entirely honest, but maybe God would forgive him that lie when he rescued the women. "It might even be nice to have a room somewhere besides the basement."

Badeau just stood there for several moments. Brian hoped he hadn't gone too far.

Finally, the captain bellowed, "Walter!"

The man hurried down the corridor toward his boss.

"Come take this man to his cell before I get angry enough to kill him."

nine

Brian's confrontation with Badeau did bring relief. The pirate must have changed his mind, because over the next three days, several items were added to the cell. Brian now had a comfortable chair and an oil lamp. Three books rested on the table beside the lamp. One of them was the Bible he had requested from Walter. Brian took comfort from the words in Psalms. He also read from the book of Samuel, which said that the battle was the Lord's. When he first saw those words, peace settled into his heart. He felt God telling him that He would win the battle. Brian wanted to tell Angelina, but how could he explain the feeling of God's presence?

Walter carried a small chest of drawers into Brian's room. It contained several changes of clothes. A washstand with a white pitcher and bowl soon rested beside the chest. The basement room began to feel more like a home than a prison. If only the door weren't kept locked.

A week later, while Brian worked beside the pirates on the house, he slipped a nail into his pocket. That night, when he was alone in his cell and the sounds of the household above him had silenced, he took out the nail and inserted it into the lock. On his knees, he worked it around and around, trying to feel for the tumblers. When he couldn't, he decided to bend the nail against the base of the bars. The nail resisted his efforts for a long time, but eventually the end of it turned to one side. By that time, Brian was exhausted. He put the nail in the bottom of one of the drawers in the chest, then went to bed. Tomorrow night he would try the nail again.

When he had supper with Badeau and the women the next day, Brian had a difficult time keeping his mind on the conversation. He could hardly wait until he could try the nail. He had to make it work.

That night, he made himself wait until the house had been quiet for a while. Then he inserted the nail into the lock. With the bent end, he could feel the tumblers. He worked and worked at them, but the pointed tip kept slipping off.

Brian stood and looked around his cell. The rocks that made up the walls might work to file off the tip, but he didn't want anyone to hear the scraping noise. After going to one of the corners of the outside wall, he knelt on the floor and dragged the nail across the bottom rock. Surely the sound would be absorbed by the earth on the other side. He repeated the task until the end of the nail was blunt.

After rushing back to the door, he tried once again to trip the tumbler. On the third try, it moved. Brian opened his cell door. He stepped from the lighted room into the darkness beyond. Thankfully, a bright moon cast its beams through the windows on one side of the basement. A feeling of freedom welled up in him as he explored the rest of the underground area.

Brian wondered if he could get into the treasure room. The only way he would chance that was if he could figure out how to relock the door when he finished. He went back to his cell, pulled the door closed, and inserted the nail. After some maneuvering, the door was fastened securely. Knowing it was late, Brian stretched out on his bunk and tried to go to sleep. He would need rest if he had to help the pirates again tomorrow.

"Good morning, Brian." Walter's voice from outside the cell woke Brian before the door opened. "Are you ready to go to breakfast?"

Brian jumped up from the bed and started splashing water on his face.

"We're going to allow the women to wash their clothes again this morning," the Englishman said.

Brian smiled. His lack of rest wouldn't be a problem if all he had to do was guard the women from the other pirates while they completed their task.

That night, he unlocked his cell once again. Carrying the oil lamp with him, he approached the door to the treasure room. After setting the lamp on the floor, he inserted the nail into the lock. This one was a little more complicated than the cell door. However, he eventually tripped the tumblers. He opened the door slowly, not wanting a squeaking hinge to alert the guards. He picked up the lamp and approached the area where the items from the *Angelina Star* were stored.

He found the strongbox from their ship. It took him awhile, but he finally got it open. The ship's papers lay on top. When he lifted them out, he discovered a large pile of coins. The money actually belonged to his employer, so if he took some of it, he wouldn't feel as if he were stealing. Arturo Fuente would want him to have what he needed to help his daughter escape.

After slipping a few gold doubloons into his pocket, he closed the lid. Relocking the strongbox took even longer than opening it, but the door to the treasure room was easier to lock. When Brian returned to his cell, he hid the money in the bottom of the chest under his clothing.

❧

Angelina dreaded supper. Although she enjoyed the other

two meals when Brian was the only man with them, she was tired of Badeau's presence. She didn't care if he did plan to end his piracy. She almost wished he would return to the sea, if only other people wouldn't be hurt by it. The man grated on her nerves.

When he was in the room, he dominated everything, including all conversation. He was so large, he made the room feel smaller. Angelina didn't like answering his intrusive questions.

She didn't like the way he always kept his eyes on her, either, as if she were on display just for him. His leering eyes made her feel as if she needed a bath. She wished she had some old, shapeless, hideous clothing that would cloak her figure and hide it from his prying gaze.

Angelina would never trust him. She had seen his barbarism on the ship. How in the world he ever thought any decent woman would want to marry him was a mystery to her.

After they had eaten the meal, Badeau asked her and Brian to accompany him out on the balcony. They stood by the railing and breathed the evening air, heavy with the earthy smell that came up from the swampy bayou. Dusk fell over the bayou before the man spoke a word.

"He says he'll be leaving in the morning." Brian's eyes bored into hers before he averted his gaze toward the treetops across the clearing. "He asked if you want him to bring you anything from New Orleans."

"I don't want anything from him." Angelina tried to keep the malice from her voice. She didn't want to anger the pirate.

"I can't tell him that." Brian turned his gaze back toward her. "What else should I say?"

"Tell him, 'No, thank you.'" Aunt Elena's voice floated out

from just inside the door, where she stood watching.

Angelina nodded to her aunt, then turned to Brian. "Yes, tell him that. We want to remain safe until my father comes after us."

❧

Angelina's words cut through Brian's heart like a sword. He was sure that by now Señor Fuente knew the ship was lost. He would have no way of knowing that any of them were alive or where to find them if they were. Brian had to do something. . .soon.

The next morning, when Walter came to take him to breakfast, Brian told him, "I want to take the Bible upstairs so I can read it to the women."

Walter glanced from the book in Brian's hand to his face. "I don't see any problem with that."

Brian and the women had just started eating breakfast when he heard Badeau's heavy footsteps in the hallway outside. He looked at Angelina and saw her face blanch. Why was the man coming to bother them at breakfast? She took a deep breath, and her face hardened into an expressionless mask.

The pirate captain strode confidently through the doorway. "I want to tell Angelina good-bye."

Brian translated his words. Angelina nodded to the man, picked up her spoon, and returned her attention to the porridge in the bowl before her.

Badeau hesitated, as if waiting for some word from her. When none came, he stomped from the room.

Angelina looked at her aunt, then turned her gaze toward Brian. Her sad eyes tugged at his heart. They glistened with tears, but she resolutely brushed them away.

"At least he won't be around for a few days." Angelina

lifted her chin higher. "We can enjoy spending three meals a day without his presence."

Brian knew that wasn't going to happen.

"Do you think the other pirates will continue working on the house while he's gone? Or will it be quieter around here for a while?" Angelina's voice sounded livelier than it had for several days.

"I don't know." Brian had other things to think about besides the construction of the house.

After they finished eating and Walter left the room, Brian opened the Bible to First Samuel, chapter seventeen, and read aloud. " 'And all this assembly shall know that the Lord saveth not with sword and spear: for the battle is the Lord's, and he will give you into our hands.' " He looked up at Angelina. "When I read these words earlier, God spoke to my heart. He assured me that He will help us win the battle over Badeau."

"How?" Angelina asked.

"He will help us get away. And I believe He will help us capture the pirates, too."

A puzzled expression covered Angelina's face, causing her brow to wrinkle. Her eyes clouded. "And how will He do that?"

"I'm not sure, but I have peace in my heart." Brian took a deep breath. "Do you trust me?"

Angelina nodded.

Elena put down her needlework and turned her attention toward Brian.

"I don't believe Badeau will harm you. I'm sure you've noticed that he has been trying to court you in the evenings. He wants you to marry him."

Elena gasped, and Angelina clasped her hands close to her throat. Brian wished he could protect her from everything, but he felt that she needed to know what Badeau had in mind. He had to escape and go for help, and he couldn't take her with him. He hoped, if she understood the pirate's plans, she wouldn't be too worried about Badeau harming her when he discovered Brian was gone.

Brian stood and paced across the room. He turned around and looked back at the women. "I'm going to escape tonight."

Angelina jumped up and rushed to him. "Take us with you." She grasped his upper arms as if they were a lifeline.

Brian gazed into her pleading eyes. This was going to be harder than he thought. He didn't want to deny her anything, but he knew there was only one way to save them. "I can travel much faster alone than if you were with me. Having the two of you along would almost guarantee our recapture. I will return as soon as possible with help."

Angelina looked stricken for a moment. Then she threw her arms around him and buried her head against his chest. "Do what you must," she whispered. "But it will be awful here without you."

☙

When the house had quieted down, Brian dressed in the darkest clothes in the chest. He stuffed a change of clothing into a pillowcase. The doubloons went into his pocket along with the nail. If he weren't afraid of waking someone, he would have gone up on the first floor to try to find the weapons room. Walter had told him about it. But he was certain Badeau kept the weapons locked up when they were at the plantation, and Brian knew he would make too much noise or take too long trying to pick the lock.

When he opened the door to his cell, the rest of the basement was in total darkness. *Good.* That meant the moon wasn't bright tonight. He took the lamp with him to help him find his way across the larger room and up the stairs to the outside door. Carefully, he inched it open and peered out. None of the pirate guards were visible on this side of the house. He let the door down softly and set in his mind exactly where he was. Then he backed down the stairs and blew out the lamp, leaving it beside the wall. After scaling the steps once again, he opened the door and slipped into the dark night.

He crept around to the front of the house, then ran across the clearing toward the trees on the side away from the bayou. All the time, his senses remained alert for the slightest sound that would signal someone was near.

He succeeded in reaching the sheltered undergrowth without detection. Earlier in the day, he had heard some of the pirates talking about slipping away to the settlement of Baton Rouge now that Badeau had gone to New Orleans. When their boss wasn't around to watch over them, they liked to frequent a pub there.

If Baton Rouge was close enough for the pirates to slip away for a drink, Brian figured he should be able to find the place, too. Perhaps he could get some help there, or at least discover a way to return to St. Augustine.

Although the moon wasn't bright, it did give enough light to help Brian find his way through the trees. He crept through the underbrush in the direction of the Mississippi. When he could see the water rippling in the waning moonlight, he kept it in sight as he made his way upriver toward the town. It couldn't be too far if the pirates went there to drink.

When dawn started to paint the sky with light, he still hadn't reached any settlement. He climbed a tall tree the way he'd climbed the rigging on the ship. Near the top, he settled into an area formed by three branches coming together on the trunk. He curled up in a ball and rested his head on the stuffed pillowcase. He would nap there until it was dark again. He hoped he wouldn't snore and alert someone to his presence.

❧

Arturo de la Fuente didn't even open the mercantile for two days after the whaling captain brought him the news about the *Angelina Star*. When he did open the store, he didn't care whether he sold anything or not. How could he go on without his Angelina?

His housekeeper, Bridgett Lawson, had done her best to get him out of his dark mood, but nothing helped. Day after day, she prepared his favorite meals, and most of them went uneaten. So she gave the food to any family she could find who needed a good meal.

"Well, now, you're just going to be a bag of bones if you don't start eating again." The woman's cheery voice didn't help him a bit. "You've got a passel of friends and customers who depend on you." She set in front of him a steaming plate piled with scrambled eggs and biscuits that Arturo knew would melt in his mouth. "Come on. You need your strength."

Arturo looked up into her smiling face and tried to return her smile. He was sure the effort didn't quite make it. "Thank you, Bridgett. What would I do without you?" He couldn't keep the plaintive tone from his voice.

She plopped down in the chair across the table. "What indeed?" Buttering her biscuit, she said, "You know, Mr.

Fuente, I wouldn't be so sure that everyone on the ship was lost. What if another ship picked up survivors but couldn't take the time to bring them home? They could be on their way even as we speak."

He knew she was trying to help, but nothing could change what had happened.

A knock on the front door interrupted the woman's conversation.

Bridgett patted him on the hand. "Now, you just sit there. I'll get it." She arose and hurried through the house.

Arturo strained to hear who was at the door, but the only sound he heard was his housekeeper's loud gasp. He jumped up and made haste to join her. "Who is it, Bridgett?"

"It's me, Señor Fuente." A voice he never expected to hear again greeted him.

Arturo grabbed the edge of the open door. "Brian?. . .Is that really you?"

The man who stood in the doorway sounded like his right-hand man, but he looked much older than when he had left for Spain about six months ago. His black hair hung longer than Arturo had ever seen it, and a brown beard covered the lower half of his face. Brian had never worn clothing like he had on now. Where had he come from, and what had happened to him? But more important. . .

"Where's my Angelina?" The words came from his throat sounding like a frog's croak.

The silence that followed his question was deafening.

Bridgett finally broke it. "Now, come right in here and join us for a bite to eat, Brian O'Doule." She led the way to the kitchen. The two men obediently followed.

Arturo slipped into his chair and leaned his shaky arms

against the side of the table. He looked up at Brian, waiting for him to answer his question.

The Irishman stood with his hands behind his back. "I have a lot to tell you, sir. Some of it good. . .some not so good."

Arturo nodded. "Go on."

"Angelina is alive and well."

The words brought jubilation to Arturo's heart. He jumped up. "Take me to her. I need to see her."

Brian cleared his throat. "That isn't possible right now."

Arturo leaned on the edge of the table, then sank back into his chair. "Why not?"

Brian's gaze darted around the room while he collected his thoughts. "Let me start at the beginning."

The story was a long one, but Arturo sat and listened without interrupting, trying to understand all he heard. Pirates. . .Angelina and Elena captured. . .Brian acting as translator. . .the sinking of the *Angelina Star*. . .a plantation in Spanish West Florida. Such a fantastic story!

"Señor Fuente." Brian slid to his knees beside Arturo's chair. "I must ask your forgiveness."

Arturo gazed at him through tears. "Why do I need to forgive you?"

Tears also glistened on the Irishman's cheeks. "I was the lookout in the crow's nest. I was distracted, and I didn't see the pirate ship soon enough to outrun her. It's all my fault."

Arturo didn't know what to think. Maybe it was Brian's fault, but maybe the pirate ship would have been too fast to outrun anyway.

"Why did you leave my Angelina at that plantation house?" His voice held accusation in it, but he didn't care.

Brian stood and pushed his hands into his front pockets. "I prayed and prayed, and I felt God leading me. We couldn't all have escaped. I don't believe Badeau will harm the women. I wanted to rescue them, but I'll need help to do that. I didn't know who I could trust in that area, so I made my way to Baton Rouge. I used one of your doubloons to buy a horse. I found a hostler who was coming to St. Augustine to pick up a coach and team for his employer, and I convinced him to let me ride along. That's the only way I could have found my way through the wilderness."

"How did you get one of my doubloons?"

Brian looked at Bridgett, then back at Arturo. "I picked the locks in the basement where they kept me locked up. Then I broke into the treasure room and took a few coins so I would have some money if I needed it. That's how I bought provisions for the trip, too. I'll pay you back the money I spent, and I'll give you what I have left." He pulled one hand out of his pocket and held up a doubloon.

Arturo stood. "I'm not worried about the money. Let's get back to figuring out how to rescue Angelina and Elena."

The two men talked a long time before Brian went home to get some rest. He would return later to finalize plans. They agreed that the only way to really be safe from Badeau would be for the governor to send his men to arrest him. Without that, the pirate might follow them and attack them as they were trying to return to St. Augustine.

Arturo's heart started to feel alive again. Angelina wasn't dead. They were going to rescue her. Brian may have been partly to blame, but Arturo didn't want to think about that now. He wanted to celebrate the fact that he hadn't lost his daughter. With a lighter step, he went to open the store.

જ

Brian had thought it would be harder to convince Señor Fuente to forgive him. The man was so glad to know his daughter still lived that he didn't seem to hold a grudge.

When Brian returned to the store the next morning, Arturo agreed to give him any help he needed. They outfitted one of Señor Fuente's ships that was already in port with everything they thought the men would need to rescue Angelina. Arturo put Brian in charge of the expedition and assigned Captain O'Rourke, the commander of his ship *St. Augustine*, to accompany him, along with his crew and several additional men.

Arturo said he would contact the governor and have him send some of his guards to New Orleans, but Brian needed to be on his way as soon as possible. The sooner they got the women out of danger, the better.

Brian stood on the deck beside the captain as they sailed south from St. Augustine, Florida. "Have you ever been in the Gulf of Mexico?"

"Yes. We sailed to New Orleans once."

"Good. That's where we need to go."

The crossing of the gulf was uneventful. The only problem they encountered was trying to find the mouth of the Mississippi. After they had finally entered that waterway and started toward the port city, Brian and the captain met for supper and a planning session.

"I was below deck in the brig when we sailed upriver," Brian said, "so I'm not sure how to get from New Orleans to the plantation house. But I heard the pirates talk about a pub in New Orleans called the Pirate's Lair. The men like to go there whenever they're in the area."

"What's your plan?" Captain O'Rourke laid his utensils beside his plate and tented his fingers.

"A couple of the men and I could dress like pirates and frequent the place until I see one of Badeau's crew. Then we could follow them back to the plantation."

O'Rourke squinted. "What about our ship? Won't they recognize that it's a merchant vessel?"

"There are lots of coves and channels off the river. We could hide in one of them and get into town on one of the smaller boats."

"This sounds like quite an adventure." The captain smiled at Brian. "Merchant captains don't get much adventure. I'll personally accompany you into New Orleans."

Brian laughed. "If it's adventure you want, I'm afraid you'll get more than you ever dreamed of."

ten

The morning after Etienne Badeau said he was going to New Orleans, Walter brought breakfast for two to the women's room. Angelina asked him in Spanish where Brian was, but the Englishman just shook his head, not understanding what she said to him.

Except when Walter brought their meals, she and Aunt Elena were alone in their rooms. No more excursions into the yard, not even to wash their clothes. Oh, how she missed Brian O'Doule. And not just because his presence allowed them to leave their room. The twinkle that always lit his eyes brought a sparkle to her life that nothing else could.

Often when Brian translated the pirate captain's words, it sounded as if Brian were speaking to her for himself. Angelina knew he wanted to protect her and Aunt Elena, but it was more than that. Something in Brian called to something in Angelina's own heart. Since he had been gone, Angelina experienced a loneliness she had never felt before. One way she felt closer to him was by reading his beloved Bible.

"Mi ángel." Aunt Elena stood in the doorway of the parlor fanning herself with her handkerchief. "What are you doing out here?"

Angelina sat in a chair on the balcony with Brian's Bible open on her lap. "I'm reading." Her right hand smoothed the corners of the pages that flapped in the breeze.

"What are you reading?" Elena glided across the floor and

leaned against the railing. "You seemed so engrossed."

Angelina smiled up at her. "Brian O'Doule had a different kind of relationship with God from the one I've had. I wanted to find out why."

Her duenna came close enough to look at the words. "Does this book tell you about it?"

"Yes." A gentle breeze once again ruffled the pages of the book in Angelina's lap. "I've always believed there is a God, and I've known Jesus was His Son; but I've never felt a connection to Him."

Aunt Elena nodded. "He's up in heaven, and we're down here, so you wouldn't feel really close to Him, now, would you?"

After closing the book, Angelina stood and joined her aunt beside the railing. "I've been reading that Jesus came to earth to die for us."

"Yes, I've heard about that."

"But He wants to be part of our lives, too." Angelina didn't know how else to express what she felt deep in her soul.

"I'm not sure I know what you mean." Aunt Elena shook her head. "How could He be part of our lives?"

Angelina turned her face into the wind to let the breeze blow through her hair. It felt almost as if someone were running their fingers through the strands. "Do you feel the wind?"

"What a silly question. How could I not? It is the only thing that keeps us from melting in this place." Aunt Elena dabbed her sticky forehead with her handkerchief.

"I can't see the wind, but I know it's here, because I feel it." Angelina picked up the book and clasped it to her chest. "When I read the words Jesus spoke when He was on earth, I feel Him around me just as much as I feel this breeze. I can almost hear His voice speak the words to my heart. I believe that's what Brian O'Doule felt, too."

Elena looked out across the yard toward the water of the bayou, which reflected the afternoon sun. "How do you get that feeling?"

"Sometimes when I read, I talk to Jesus. One day, I told Him that I want Him to be a part of my life. I want to follow Him."

"Do you think it did any good?" Aunt Elena started through the door. "If Jesus wants to help us, He can let Brian rescue us from this place."

"He will." Angelina followed her into the parlor.

"We don't even know if Brian is still alive." Aunt Elena dropped onto a settee and picked up her needlework. "The pirates have been searching for him every day, but they obviously haven't found any sign of him. None of the small boats are missing, so he couldn't have escaped." She set to work with a vengeance, punching her needle into and out of the fabric.

If Brian had managed to get away, maybe they would be rescued soon. But what if he lost his way in the wilderness or one of the pirates found him? If it wasn't so dangerous to let Walter know that she spoke English, she could give him a letter for her father and ask him to mail it for her. Perhaps she could convince him without talking to him.

Angelina sat at the desk and dipped the pen in the inkwell. She quickly filled a page of parchment. She described the pirate's attack on the *Angelina Star* and explained how Brian O'Doule had protected them and helped them. She told him she was sure she would soon see him again. Then she closed the missive with sealing wax. It was almost time for supper.

She hoped Walter would accept the letter and post it for her.

❧

In the early evening, a glow from the lights of New Orleans beckoned around a bend in the Mississippi. Brian stood on the quarterdeck of the *St. Augustine* beside Captain O'Rourke. He pointed out a place on the riverbank where the dark path of water led toward a break between the trees. "That would be a good place to take the ship, wouldn't it?"

After agreeing, the skipper gave orders to his men. Because the holds of the merchant ship were empty, it rode high in the water, making it easy to skim between the sand bars that lined the closer banks of the small tributary. A little farther into the channel, the water widened into a pleasant cove overhung with branches. O'Rourke turned into it and dropped anchor.

"Should we make our way into town tonight?" The captain sounded eager, ready for action.

Brian shook his head, though he hated to disappoint the man. "It would be easier to go in the daylight since we don't know what we're looking for. And we don't want to draw undue attention to ourselves."

Waiting wasn't something Brian liked to do. Here he was, so close to Angelina, yet so far away. What hurdles stood between him and rescuing the woman he loved? He knew he should go down to his bunk and get some sleep, but restlessness kept him on deck long into the night. Just how far was it to the plantation house from New Orleans? He could only guess since he had been in the brig when they made the journey upriver last time.

What was happening with Angelina and her aunt? Had Badeau taken his anger out on them when the man found out that he had escaped? Brian gazed at the stars twinkling in the sky. *Please, Father God, keep the women safe. Don't let Badeau hurt them because of me. And please help us find the place we need tomorrow.*

❧

When Walter brought their breakfast, Angelina smiled at the Englishman. She thanked him in Spanish for all he did for them. The way he nodded, she was sure he understood her intent if not her words.

After they were finished eating, Walter returned for the dishes. Before he could put them on his tray, Angelina pulled the letter from her pocket and held it out to him. He looked at it as if it were a snake that would bite him. He shook his head, refusing to take the paper in her hand.

"Por favor, señor," she pleaded.

He gave his head a more vigorous shake and began gathering the dishes onto the tray.

Angelina touched his arm. He jerked back as if he had been burned. Undaunted, she thrust the paper toward him. This time he took it, but instead of putting it in his pocket, he tore it into pieces. He left the scraps of paper on the table, then exited.

Tears of disappointment filled Angelina's eyes. Walter had always treated her and Aunt Elena with great respect. She had begun to think he felt sorry for their plight. But she must have been mistaken. Or maybe he was afraid that if Badeau ever found out, he would be severely punished. After all, hadn't Brian escaped while Walter was in charge?

Angelina picked up the pieces of parchment and Brian's Bible. She tucked each piece between the pages and bowed her head over the holy book. Their only hope now was God.

A cock's crow somewhere on the banks of the river signaled the dawn. Brian felt as if he had just laid his head on the hard pillow, but he opened his eyes and sat up. Today could be the day when he would be able to return to Angelina at the plantation house. After dressing, he met the captain on deck.

"Do you have our day planned out?" The skipper studied Brian's expression.

"It would probably be best if we took a small boat and posed as fishermen until we reach New Orleans. Do we have one without a name painted on the side?"

O'Rourke pointed to two small boats resting on deck, their oars beside them. "How many people should go?"

Brian judged the size of the overturned dinghy. "I don't think more than two or three. Do you have any fishing equipment?"

"We always keep a few poles and hooks." O'Rourke nodded toward where the poles were tied against the wall.

The captain asked his men to bring their sea chests on deck. He explained to the crew what they needed to do. Then he and Brian went through the chests to find the clothes they would need as they masqueraded as fishermen and then as pirates. None of the men had shaved since they left St. Augustine, so their beards would fit right in with either of the roles.

When Brian finished dressing in fisherman's clothes and filling a kit bag with the pirate disguise, he looked down at himself. He had worn rough clothing all those years he had been a sailor before he worked for Señor Fuente. Sometimes he wore older clothes when he worked in the warehouse, but he had gotten used to dressing like a gentleman. Looking like this, he felt as if he were going backward instead of moving ahead in his life. But he didn't mind. He didn't even care if some people thought he was an outlaw. Nothing was more important than his mission.

When the three men reached New Orleans, they would shed their fisherman's clothing and don the pirate disguises. Most of the people they came into contact with there would likely think they were outlaws. They certainly wouldn't be able to mingle with polite society. But Brian didn't care. Everything would be worth it when he was able to rescue Angelina and her aunt, removing them from the clutches of the evil pirate.

Soon Brian, the captain, and a sailor named Murphy were in the small boat, headed upriver toward New Orleans. Murphy rowed while the other two men tried to catch some fish. If they had a few in the boat when they arrived on shore, that would keep people from becoming suspicious.

As it turned out, no one seemed to take much notice of the three men when they tied up at the wharf. The waterfront of New Orleans was like that of any port—dirty, smelling of rotting fish, and with riffraff loitering about, watching other people work.

After slipping into an empty alleyway and switching into the pirate clothing, the men made their way through a quiet section of the city. When they moved beyond the sights and sounds of the waterfront, stores and shops dotted the sides of the streets. As Brian looked down one of the thoroughfares, he noticed homes behind tall iron fences several blocks away. He wondered how far they would have to go to find a place to sleep while keeping vigil for the pirates.

After wandering the streets for over an hour, the trio turned a corner and saw just what they sought. A carved wooden sign proclaiming PIRATE'S LAIR hung from a signpost in front of an English-style pub. Brian nodded to the two other men. "There it is."

"Should we go in together?" O'Rourke asked.

Brian gave it a moment's thought. "Maybe not. We won't draw as much attention if we wander in at different times."

Brian went in first. He pulled his hat down to shadow his face and stepped into the smoky interior. A huge fireplace on one wall contained a smoldering log. He walked up to the bar and asked if they served breakfast.

"What's your pleasure?" The man behind the counter stopped drying the mug he held in his hand. "Ale and porridge perhaps?"

Brian shook his head. "Too early in the morning for ale. How's your water?"

The man cackled. "I'd stick to the ale."

Soon after Brian sat at one of the long tables, O'Rourke came in with Murphy. After they obtained some bread and cheese from the man behind the counter, they sat at the other end of the table from Brian. All three men kept their heads down and looked as if they were concentrating on their food. Brian took furtive glances at all the people in the room, keeping his ears open to catch any word that might lead them to Badeau or any of the pirates with him.

By midmorning, each of the three men had sauntered out of the pub and walked down the block to their prearranged meeting place. O'Rourke looked wound up as tight as a seven-day clock. "Nothing happened, did it?"

"It may take time," Brian tried to reassure him.

The captain scratched his chin. "You said the plantation was quite a ways up the river. Maybe we should buy a fishing boat that's large enough for sails. It could take a long time to row upriver against the current. The pirates might get away from us."

Brian nodded. He had been trying not to spend too much of Señor Fuente's money. But he knew the man would want them to do whatever it took to rescue his daughter.

The men proceeded to the wharf. They sauntered along the waterfront, making small talk about fishing while keeping an eye on the boats for sale. When they found one that met their needs, they purchased it and moved it to the dock beside their dinghy.

Brian felt good about the deal they made. They hadn't spent nearly as much money as he had anticipated. "After we find a place to stay, we can work out a rotation. Someone should be in the pub around the clock, so we'll sleep in shifts."

They found a squatty inn a couple of blocks up the street from the pub, and Brian rented a second-floor room. He hoped they wouldn't need it more than a day or two.

O'Rourke took the first shift in the pub. Murphy would follow him. Brian went up to the room. Before he slipped into bed, he spent time on his knees.

Father God, we can't do this without Your help. Please protect the captain and Murphy from detection. Hold Angelina and her aunt close to Your heart and protect them from any harm.

eleven

A bellowing voice shouting English words with a French accent announced to Angelina that Etienne Badeau had returned. Evidently Walter had told him that Brian had escaped.

"What do you mean, he's not here?" The pirate captain's voice was even louder than before.

Walter gave a long explanation, but his words were too subdued to understand.

"Assemble all the men on the front lawn." Badeau's words echoed through the house.

Angelina stayed inside the room but peeked around the window facing and watched the men hurrying to obey the captain's commands. Most of them looked frightened. After a long, animated discussion, Badeau told Walter to dismiss the men. Then he strode toward the house. Angelina moved back so he would not see her spying on them.

"What is happening, mi ángel?" Fright covered Aunt Elena's face.

Angelina went to her companion and put her arms around the older woman. "Badeau has returned. I believe he knows Brian is gone."

Elena sat on one of the couches and picked up a pillow top she had just started working on the day before. The repetitive work seemed to keep her aunt from losing control of her emotions in crisis situations.

Moments later, Angelina heard heavy footsteps ascend the

stairs and stop outside the door.

"Walter," the captain hollered, "bring the key!"

Angelina held her breath.

The door opened without the usual knock. Badeau strode into the room, followed by Walter. The Englishman stood with shoulders slumped, hands clasped in front of him. Angelina had never seen him look so cowed.

"Do these women know where the Irishman is?" Badeau asked in English.

Angelina kept her features emotionless to keep from letting the man know that she understood what he said.

"We could not find out what they know. No one here speaks Spanish." Walter bowed his head slightly.

Badeau paced toward the open doors of the balcony. He leaned his huge hands on the door facings, his glare turned toward the view outside, but Angelina could see the tight set of his jaw muscles.

She perched on the edge of the settee and folded her hands in her lap. She clasped them together to keep them from quivering. Nothing could still her heart and stomach.

Badeau turned and stared at her. She lowered her eyes, but peeked out from under her lids.

"Are the women scared of me?" the captain asked.

Walter shrugged. "You have been shouting a lot this morning."

Badeau gave a snort. "I won't hurt the women. I haven't changed my mind about marrying the younger one."

Angelina couldn't keep her hands from shaking. She was glad the captain was looking at Walter, because she knew it would anger him even more if he saw her reaction.

"Have the men found any trace of the Irishman?"

Angelina eagerly awaited the answer.

"No, Etienne. Nothing."

Her heart sank.

Badeau laughed. "He knows nothing about this country. One of the gators probably had him for supper."

He came to stand near Angelina. She stared at his boots in front of her. To her surprise, his large hand touched her chin, raising it gently until she was looking up at the man's face. His smile twinkled along with the gold in his teeth.

"I need to talk to her." Badeau removed his hand and turned toward Walter. "Are you sure there is no one on the crew who speaks Spanish?"

Walter shook his head. "No one."

"Then send a man into town and find someone who does."

"Whatever you say, Etienne."

Angelina realized she had been holding her breath ever since the man touched her. She slowly released it, trying not to make any noise. She glanced at Aunt Elena and saw that her face was as white as the cloth she worked on. Angelina hoped her companion wouldn't faint before the men left.

"I have some gifts for Angelina. Let's go get them." Badeau led the way out the door, and Walter locked it behind them.

Angelina wilted against the back of the settee and placed one hand over her eyes. *Father God, please protect us until Brian returns.* Somehow, in her heart, she couldn't believe that Brian was dead. She still felt a connection with him, even though he wasn't present.

Later that day, Etienne Badeau came back to their room. Walter accompanied him, carrying four new dresses. The pirate captain watched as Walter laid them over one of the chairs. He presented them to Angelina one at a time.

Afraid to reject them, she ran her fingers over the fabric and admired the colors and textures. Each one was a different color, all of them lavishly decorated with lace. They weren't suitable for day wear. They could only be worn for parties or a dress-up dinner. She tried to smile her thanks, but she knew that if the pirate looked into her eyes, he would see that the smile was insincere. Thankfully, he didn't get that close.

Later, when Walter brought their evening meal, Badeau arrived with him. As the captain studied Angelina, his expression indicated he was disappointed about something. She didn't know what until she heard him whisper to Walter that she was not wearing one of her new dresses.

Although they ate together, there could be no conversation between them. Angelina tried to act as if she were enjoying his company, but she had a hard time forcing the food down her throat, which was tight from unshed tears. When she peeked at Aunt Elena, she saw her duenna moving her spoon around in the rich broth of the turtle soup.

Eventually, the men left the women alone.

The next day, Badeau and Walter brought Angelina a string of pearls along with earrings, a ring, and a bracelet to match. When Walter laid them in her lap, she fingered their smooth surfaces, wondering whether he had bought them or if some woman somewhere was yearning for her lost jewelry. She wished the man would stop bringing her gifts. She didn't know how to react to keep from making him angry. But she knew she could never place them on her body.

Early the next morning, Angelina went out on the balcony to read the Bible. Moments later, she heard Badeau and Walter on the porch below, their voices drifting up to her.

"What is wrong with Miles?" Badeau sounded as if he really cared.

"He hasn't been happy since you captured the women." Walter hesitated, then continued. "He thought you should just kill everyone. Then you took his cabin on the ship. You've made him work on this house, and he only wants to be a sailor. Now you're in a foul mood since you can't communicate with the women."

"She accepted the gifts I gave her, but she hasn't used any of them." The captain's voice sounded closer, so Angelina guessed he must have stood. "I thought she would wear one of the dresses or at least put on the jewelry. Wouldn't most women be glad to receive such nice things?"

"I'm sure they would. But you can't take it out on the men. Miles is threatening to leave. He probably would have by now if you had divided the loot with them."

"That's why I haven't done it yet. I want to keep the men here until everything is finished."

The next words were quieter; Angelina figured the two men must be entering the house.

She closed the Bible and bowed her head. In the stillness of the morning, she poured her heart out to her heavenly Father. When she fell silent to wait for Him, a sweet voice spoke to her heart. *Wait for now. I am in control.*

A new hope sparked to life and burned in her heart.

❧

For three days, Brian and his friends kept the Pirate's Lair pub under surveillance. He tired of the monotony. Sleeping, eating, walking around the city that was sleepy in the daytime and jumping at night. Sometimes he talked to God while he walked, always lifting up Angelina and Elena, praying for their protection. He hoped he and his shipmates would find the pirates soon. But he knew it might take awhile before any of them would come to New Orleans.

Shortly after Murphy sauntered out the door of the pub, Brian went in. He ordered a bowl of stew and hot corn bread. Darkness was rapidly descending outside the open door. He slathered butter on the hot bread and sank his teeth into it. By the time he finished chewing, two men came in from the street. They ordered tankards of ale and brought them to sit at the other end of the long table from Brian.

He glanced up and almost dropped his spoon in the bowl. One of the men was Miles Henderson, Badeau's first mate. Pulling his hat brim lower over his eyes, Brian turned away. He hadn't recognized the other man, but when the sailor spoke, Brian remembered hearing his voice outside his cell on the pirate ship. Finally, they were getting somewhere. That is, if these two men were still with Badeau.

The longer they drank, the louder their voices became.

"All Etienne thinks about is that woman." The sailor with the first mate sounded angry.

"Too bad he can't talk to her anymore." Henderson threw back his head and laughed. "Actually, I'm glad the Irishman escaped. Badeau had things too easy. It's time something didn't go his way. He tries to control everyone around him. At least he can't control the women—except for keeping them locked up."

The other man joined the laughter, then ordered another round of drinks.

Their shared confidences and tales grew louder and longer, filling the tavern with unbelievable stories that everyone in the room could hear. Henderson leaned his arms on the table as if he was having trouble staying upright. His mate propped his elbow on the table and rested his chin in his hand just to hold his head up. He lifted the tankard with the other hand and took long swigs of the bitter ale. The men looked as if they would be drinking most of the night if they didn't fall into a drunken stupor.

"You think Badeau will figure out we're gone?" The nameless sailor set his tankard on the table, sloshing some of the ale out of it.

Henderson gave a snort of derision. "I don't care. I've half a mind to make Walter open the treasure room for us when we get back. Part of the loot belongs to us, after all. If we got our hands on what's rightfully ours, we wouldn't have to take orders from that man any longer. If he didn't dole out just a little bit of money at a time, most of us wouldn't keep working for him. We're sailors, not carpenters. And I, for one, want to get back out to sea."

Brian finished the last of his stew and rose from his chair. Slipping out the door into the heavy night air, he hurried toward the inn. O'Rourke met him halfway there.

"Two of Badeau's men are in the pub," Brian whispered. "I think they'll be there awhile, but you never know for sure."

O'Rourke fell into step beside Brian as they headed back toward the pub. "How about if I wait across the street?" the skipper said. "If they come out, follow them so I'll know who they are. We can take turns following them. They might get suspicious if they see us together."

"That sounds good to me." Brian shook the other man's hand and left him on the street corner. Then he returned to the noisy pub, sat at his table, and pretended to drink a tankard of ale.

The place grew even louder and smokier as the night went on.

By the time the two men got up to leave, they were both so drunk they were unsteady on their feet. They had a hard time maneuvering through the tables. Henderson almost fell into another rowdy patron's lap, but he caught the edge of the table just in time. The patron tried to start a fight, but his drinking buddies stopped him. When the two pirates reached the entrance, they were holding each other up.

Finally, they staggered out the door and shuffled down the boardwalk, with Brian following at a discreet distance. He glanced across the street. Two men slouched in the shadows where he had left O'Rourke. Evidently the skipper had returned to the inn and brought Murphy back with him. Brian stayed on the pub side of the street and ambled the same direction the pirates were going. Across the street, his two shipmates moved toward the wharf, too.

After the pirates fell into their small boat, they fumbled with the sail. It took them several minutes to raise it. Soon they were in the middle of the Mississippi River, making their way upstream. Brian could only hope they would return to the plantation.

He and his two friends climbed into their own boat, which was moored quite a ways down the wharf from the pirates. Brian and O'Rourke made a show of using the fishing poles while Murphy manned the sail, keeping the noisy pirates in view. The drunken sailors weren't making very fast headway, so the sailing was easy.

Brian and O'Rourke kept their fishing lines in the water while the boats made their way upriver. They didn't have any bait, so they wouldn't catch anything, but the pirates wouldn't know that—if they even noticed the other boat. Occasionally, Brian and O'Rourke saw a small boat near the bank of the river with fishing poles dropped into the water, so they fit right in.

The sun was nearing the middle of the sky when the pirates' boat turned toward the right riverbank. Murphy brought their boat close to the shore before they reached the same place. Brian sat facing upriver so he could watch the other boat. It slipped out of sight behind some trees on the bank.

After the two men pulled their lines out of the water, Murphy sailed toward the place where the pirates' boat had disappeared. Just before they reached the spot, Brian saw the bayou that emptied into the Mississippi. "That's the entrance," he said. "Pull in here."

Murphy sailed to the riverbank. The three men maneuvered the front of the boat up on the dirt.

Brian stood on the bank and studied the terrain, trying to burn it into his brain. They'd passed several similar areas. How could they find this particular one again?

Murphy tied the boat to a tree. "We need to mark this spot."

"But how?" Brian scanned everything around them, trying to find something that was different from the rest of the wilderness.

"Let's sail a bit past this point and mark a couple of trees," O'Rourke suggested.

They slid the boat back into the water and sailed it a little ways upriver from the spot where the pirates had disappeared. After tying their boat to a tree, they walked back toward the bayou. Tall trees grew along the bank. A multitude of smaller trees and bushes crowded around their trunks. The men chose two trees that were so close together their roots were probably intertwined. After removing all the brush undergrowth on the river side of the trees, they cut a wide notch into each trunk close to the ground. The notches could be seen from the river but not by anyone on land. And as low as the notches were, a person would have to be looking for them to notice they were there.

When they finished, the three men walked back into the covering growth. Brian's heartbeat accelerated. Finally, they were close to where Angelina was being held. His inclination was to rush to her, but he knew that wouldn't work. There were too many pirates around. Still, it felt good to finally be so close to reaching their goal. Turning to the other men, he smiled.

"We need to be extremely careful. And we need a plan. I have an idea about what we should do."

twelve

Angelina welcomed Walter's knock on the door, even though it meant Etienne Badeau would once again share a meal with them. At least now she was able to eat her food with the man in the room. It had taken her awhile to convince herself that she couldn't let him affect her ability to gain sustenance. She wanted to keep up her strength so that when Brian came to rescue them, she wouldn't hamper the chance to escape. She was a little worried about Aunt Elena, though. Her companion might not be able to make the getaway with them. Every day she ate less and became more frail and wan. Angelina felt sure she had given up hope.

"Thank you, Walter." Badeau smiled at the Englishman, then took his place on the settee across from Angelina and her aunt. "You may stay and eat with us."

Walter's eyes widened. This was the first time his boss had extended such an invitation. Badeau glanced at him and gestured toward the couch beside him. "You can sit here."

"I didn't bring enough food."

Badeau waved his hand toward the door. "Go get yours and come back." He turned to smile at Angelina.

She wondered what he was up to. The pirate captain seemed to operate on whims. She gave him a tight smile, inclining her head in a questioning nod. This might not be a bad thing. Maybe the two men would talk to each other and she could find out what was going on outside this room.

Walter returned with a full plate and sat beside his boss. While Angelina consumed the meal, she listened unobtrusively to the two men's conversation.

"I haven't seen Miles around lately." Badeau took a drink from the tankard beside his plate, then swiped the back of his hand across his lips.

"He's sleeping this evening, sir." Walter toyed with his roast without looking up.

"Is he sick?"

"I don't believe so." Walter grimaced. "I think he's drunk."

Badeau thumped the table with his fist, making Aunt Elena jump. "Are you letting them have too much ale?"

The Englishman gulped. "No, sir. They must have gotten it somewhere else."

Badeau sat back, ignoring his food. "They aren't supposed to go anywhere without letting me know. I may have to replace that man. He's becoming too insolent for his own good."

"It could be difficult to find a first mate who is as experienced as he is." Walter gulped some of the water from his glass, then set it back on the table. "Give him another chance. After all, he isn't a carpenter or builder, and that's what you've had the men doing while we're here."

Badeau furrowed his brow as if lost in thought. "The house is finished, so I don't need their help here anymore. But I'm waiting for a message from one of our contacts. Depending on what he tells me, we might make one more foray on the ocean. Then I'll give the men their share of the treasure and they can be on their way."

Angelina wondered what kind of foray he was talking about. She hoped he wasn't going to attack another ship. He had promised he would stop being a pirate. Too many people had already suffered at his hands.

๛

"We'll need the ship close by in case we need to make a quick getaway," Brian pointed out to Murphy and O'Rourke. "A large ship could easily overtake this little fishing boat."

O'Rourke nodded and shooed an insect from the back of his neck. "I'll have Murphy take me back. You can stay near the plantation if you want."

Brian hadn't thought of that, but it was a good idea. He could hide in the woods and keep the house under surveillance. Maybe he would even catch a glimpse of Angelina, though he didn't know if he could stand seeing her from afar and not going to her immediately.

The other two men took the fishing boat into the river. Sailing with the current, they would make good time to New Orleans. They should be back quickly. Brian waved as they rounded a bend in the mighty river.

He decided to wait until almost dark to make his way closer to the house. Waiting was the hard part, and he needed to get some rest. After climbing a tall tree, he found a place where he could lean against the trunk and have his body cradled by two adjoining limbs. He hoped he wouldn't snore.

He didn't sleep soundly. Every snap and crack in the forest woke him. But he dozed enough to refresh himself. The breeze that blew through the canopy of foliage kept him cool. Once an alligator made its noisy way through the underbrush, then slipped into the bayou with hardly a splash. Brian hadn't seen any of the huge creatures in the water of the Mississippi. Maybe they stayed in the bayous and swamps, where the movement of the water wasn't as swift.

In an adjoining tree, an opossum crouched on a branch and quinted at Brian. He thought they only came out at night. Maybe the noisy alligator had disturbed its rest, too.

Brian looked down toward a dead tree that had fallen partway into the bayou. Two large turtles lumbered out of the water and walked halfway up the length of the trunk before hunkering down in the warm late-afternoon sunlight. A crane flew from a tree on the opposite bank of the bayou and swooped toward a spot in the middle of the pool. When it came back up, a fish squirmed in its bill. Seeing that reminded Brian of how long it had been since he ate. With a growl, his stomach lurched. When he descended from the tree, he could look for edible berries.

As the day waned, the forest came alive with chirps, whirs, and scuffling as the animals moved around. A stronger wind rustled through the leaves on the trees and bushes. Maybe all this noise would cover any he would make as he moved closer to the house.

After shimmying most of the way down the trunk, Brian lost his hold on the bark and fell the last few feet. He lay still in the underbrush, waiting to see if his ungraceful landing had given his presence away. When all he heard was the continued forest sounds, he gingerly rose to his feet and glanced around to get his bearings. He sneaked from tree to tree toward the plantation house. On the way, he didn't see anything he could eat.

When the structure came into sight, he stopped to appreciate its beauty. He hadn't looked back at the house when he made his escape weeks ago, so he hadn't realized that the building had reached completion. What a shame such a lovely plantation belonged to an outlaw. Surely God wouldn't let the man start living as a decent, law-abiding citizen after all he'd done. If the governor's men were able to capture Badeau, what would happen to this wonderful place? A woman like Angelina should live in a house like this, but not with such a vile man as Badeau.

Brian crept closer, keeping an eye out for pirates. He climbed a tree with thick branches that could hide him while allowing him to observe everything that happened on this side of the house. At least he was near the rooms where Angelina and Elena were being held. . .if Badeau hadn't moved them.

The door to the balcony opened, and Angelina stepped into the evening air. Brian almost gasped. He had missed her so much, his heart hurt from the longing. Her breathtaking beauty had not dimmed in the time he had been gone, but he noticed a look of greater maturity on her face. Brian prayed it was her strength during the crisis that put it there. How he wanted to let her know that he was near, but it wasn't yet time. He had to be patient awhile longer.

Elena came through the door. Angelina helped her to a chair. Brian couldn't believe how frail the older woman looked—not at all the robust person he had last seen. His heart almost broke for what they must have suffered. It was all he could do to keep from jumping down from his perch and running to the women. But that wouldn't help them, and it might bring destruction.

❧

"Angelina." Aunt Elena's voice was almost a whisper. "I don't know how much longer I can stand to be near that man. I'm ready to give up."

"No." Angelina's vehement reply was louder than she

ntended, so she lowered her voice. She didn't want any of
he pirates to wonder what was wrong and come investigate.
I know Brian O'Doule is alive. He *is* going to rescue us."

Elena put her needlework beside her on the settee, crossed
ser arms over her waist, and clutched at her elbows. "But he's
been gone so long. Surely he would have returned by now if
se were still alive."

Angelina turned from looking out the window at the
waning daylight. She couldn't let her aunt continue having
such negative thoughts. "O my God, I trust in thee: let me
not be ashamed, let not mine enemies triumph over me."
She smiled at her aunt. "Remember how much this verse has
meant to us. We must trust God."

"But bad things happen to good people." Aunt Elena
looked so forlorn, Angelina's heart hurt as if a dagger had
pierced it.

"We've been reading the Bible together. Doesn't it give you
any hope?"

Her duenna looked up at her with a bleak expression in her
eyes. "I don't have as much hope as you do."

Angelina knelt beside her aunt. "My hope was rekindled
when I asked Jesus into my heart. I wish you would do that,
too. Then you wouldn't feel so defeated." She pulled her
aunt into her arms, and the woman wept quietly against her
shoulder.

Angelina helped her companion into her bedroom and
assisted her in preparing for bed. After Aunt Elena was
under the covers, Angelina knelt beside her and prayed until
the older woman fell asleep.

She blew out the lamps and went back out on the balcony.
Leaning against one of the support columns, she gazed into

the inky sky sparkling with a million stars that looked like diamonds. Even though they were in the wilderness, this place held a quiet beauty. The peace that came with the night invaded her soul, bringing words of praise to God into her mind. She didn't say them out loud, because one of the pirates might be out there in the darkness, and she didn't want him to know that she was outside.

On the ship, she had often heard exclamations from the sailors that contained extremely coarse language, using some words she had never heard before in her life. By the way the men said them, she knew they were bad. That language continued here at the plantation. And every time one of the pirate sailors caught sight of her or Aunt Elena, his leering expression made her want to hide in a closet. Ever since Brian's escape, she had tried to stay out of their sight, except for Walter and Badeau, of course. She couldn't hide from them.

Masculine voices invaded her silence. Badeau and Walter were once again conversing on the porch below her.

"Who were you talking to in the dining hall this afternoon?" Angelina had often heard the Englishman speak his mind to his captain.

"He's the contact I told you about."

Angelina wondered what kind of message he received.

"Did he bring good news?"

Angelina held her breath.

"Yes. When I was in New Orleans, I heard a rumor of a ship carrying a rich bounty across the Atlantic. I sent the man to find out the truth, because I don't want to chase phantoms."

Angelina heard shuffling on the porch below. Then Walter spoke again. "I thought you were going to end your life as a pirate."

"I am, my friend. But I can't pass up this last one. According reports, no other vessel has ever carried as much wealth its hold. Capturing it would be the crowning event of my reer on the high seas." Badeau's laugh echoed into the dark ght.

Angelina shivered. She had never trusted the giant pirate, ut this news made her more determined than ever to cape—with or without Brian O'Doule's help. If Aunt Elena ren't so weak, Angelina would escape tonight and take her ances in the wilderness.

"What about the women?" Walter asked.

"While I'm gone, you, the cook, and four of the sailors will ke turns guarding them. I'll leave you in charge."

Angelina wondered what Walter thought of that, but the vo men went into the house without saying anything more at she could hear.

❧

lthough the moon wasn't full, it gave enough light for rian to make out the movements of the pirate guards. After atching them for a couple of hours, he figured out their atrolling routine.

Four men took positions within sight of Brian's hiding pot. One leaned against a tree, smoking a pipe. Another ipped down to a sitting position on the ground. After a ew minutes, his head dropped to his chest as if he were sleep. The other two carried on an animated conversation ar enough away to keep from disturbing the others. Brian igured he could probably sneak into the house without nyone detecting him, but he decided to wait and see what appened tomorrow. He didn't want to take a chance on utting the women in danger.

He slept fitfully, nestled in the tree. Knowing Angeline was so close kept his nerves tingling all night.

At dawn, activity below him drew his attention. The pirate crew had assembled on the front lawn, and Badeau was talking to them. Brian was able to hear an occasional word or two, but he couldn't tell what was being said. Badeau and most of the crew headed toward the dock at the bottom of the hill. Walter and three other men stayed by the house.

The pirates who were leaving made enough noise that Brian could descend from the tree and follow them through the undergrowth without being heard. He overheard Badeau telling the other pirates that they were going out to capture another ship. Apparently the captain was lying when he said he was going to stop his life of piracy. Brian had never liked the man, and this reinforced his feelings. Etienne Badeau couldn't be trusted.

When they reached the dock, Brian saw two dinghies tied there. The pirates boarded the small boats and headed toward the schooner. Badeau sat in the front of the first dinghy, as if eager to reach his ship.

As Brian watched, the boats returned for the rest of the crew. It took several trips to bring them all. After all the men were deposited on the ship, both dinghies returned to the dock, and the two rowers went back up to the house. Brian counted the men as they boarded. By his calculations, only six men were left at the plantation.

He worked his way back through the underbrush toward the Mississippi, wondering where O'Rourke and Murphy were with the merchant ship. He hoped Badeau didn't meet them coming up the river.

By the time Brian reached the tree where he had rested the day before, he was exhausted. Too many hours without sleep left him unable to continue on. He climbed the tree to take a quick rest. The next thing he knew, a squirrel landed on his stomach, startling him awake to the early evening light. He jumped, and the animal scrambled away, leaping from the limb of Brian's tree to an adjacent one. Then it turned and chattered at him.

"Don't worry," Brian whispered. "I'm not going to hurt you." He felt foolish talking to a wild animal. It had been too long since he had a person to talk to. Maybe he could sneak into the house and see Angelina tonight.

He looked down and across the river, hoping to catch sight of Señor Fuente's ship. It wasn't there. Brian climbed down from the tree and moved closer to where the pirate ship had been anchored before Badeau boarded it. The cove was empty. Brian moved toward the plantation house and kept watch from the bushes.

Two men patrolled the grounds, one at the front of the house, the other at the back. They sat on the ground, leaning against tree trunks. It would be easy to get past these guards.

As she had the evening before, Angelina came out on the balcony and looked up at the stars. Not wanting to startle her, Brian sneaked toward a tree near the end of the balcony. Careful to be quiet, he shimmied up the trunk. He inched out onto the largest limb that pointed toward the house, testing with each step to make sure the branch was strong enough to hold his weight.

"*Pssst*," he hissed.

Angelina looked around.

As he moved farther out on the limb, it began to sway. "Please don't make any noise," he whispered.

Angelina turned and saw him. Her eyes widened, and she covered her mouth with one hand as if to keep any sound from escaping.

Even though the branch was getting much smaller, he moved closer to the house. "I'm going to drop onto the balcony."

Angelina looked out into the darkness. "Where are the guards?"

"They can't see this spot from where they're sitting." Brian took hold of the branch with both hands and dropped until his body hung suspended below it. He swung his feet a couple of times until he could grasp the closest pillar with his legs.

She moved closer. "Do you need my help?"

"No. I can make it." When he let go of the branch, he launched his upper body toward the column and wrapped his arms around it. After clinging to it for a moment, he slipped down until his legs touched the railing.

Angelina stood beside him and gave him her hand to help him down. As soon as his feet were planted on the floor, he swept her into his arms and cradled her against his chest. Her dainty hands grasped the front of his shirt, and she began to weep.

"*Shh*," he whispered against her hair. "I'm here now."

After a moment, she looked up at him. "I knew you would come back. God gave me the assurance that you would, even though the pirates decided you'd been eaten by an alligator."

Brian placed his hands on either side of her face and drank in her beauty. "Maybe it's a good thing they thought that. It kept them from hunting me down."

Her eyes seemed to devour his face, too. "You look different."

He rubbed one side of his jaw. "I darkened my beard to keep the pirates from recognizing me in New Orleans." He pulled her back into his arms.

"Badeau is going to attack another ship on the Atlantic."

Brian stepped back and took her by the shoulders. "That's a good thing. If Badeau is gone for a while, we'll have time to get you and your aunt out of here. I have one of your father's ships and crew with me. I'm waiting for them to come up from New Orleans. When they arrive, we can easily take the six men who are left here. By the time Badeau and the rest of his men come back from their raid, the governor's men will be here waiting for them."

Angelina shivered. Brian hoped she wasn't too cold. He pulled her back into his arms and rested his chin on top of her head.

"So my father knows about the attack and kidnapping." She whispered the words against his shirt.

"He heard about the ship going down. He was mourning your death when I arrived in St. Augustine. Now he awaits your return." Brian couldn't stop himself from dropping a kiss into her hair. He knew he didn't have a right to, but he had waited so long, and she willingly came into his arms. Maybe she would forgive his transgression.

He turned her face up and studied her eyes. "I can't stay here."

"I know. But just knowing you are out there keeping watch over me and Aunt Elena gives me a feeling of peace." She clutched his shirt with both hands. "You will be careful, won't you, Brian?"

He liked the sound of his name on her lips. All he could do was nod before he moved away and started climbing over the railing into the dark shadows below.

thirteen

Once again, Brian slept in the treetops on the bank of the Mississippi River. Dreams danced in his head all night long. Angelina on the *Angelina Star*, Etienne Badeau's angry face, Señor Fuente when he found out the daughter he thought dead was still alive, Angelina slipping into Brian's embrace. He leaned down to bury his face in the hair on top of her head and awoke with a start, probably from the sound of his stomach's fierce growling. If he didn't get something to eat soon, he would lose too much strength. After stretching his muscles, he lowered himself down the tree. He could already feel some weakness as he grasped the trunk. He lost his hold before he reached the bottom. The impact with the hard ground did nothing to ease his aches and pains.

He bent over, braced his hands on his knees, and took several deep breaths. After straightening, he peeked through the underbrush toward the river. The musty smell of damp leaves carpeting the ground rose in the summer heat. Not far away, he spotted the *St. Augustine*, Señor Fuente's merchant ship, coming upriver toward him, the fishing boat tied behind it. *Finally!*

Brian stepped between the bushes and waved with both arms to get Captain O'Rourke's attention. After signaling back, the captain pointed toward the bayou. Brian gave him an affirmative salute. The ship pulled out of the flow of the river, and Captain O'Rourke dropped the anchor in the more tranquil pool. Soon he and Murphy had a dinghy in the water headed toward where Brian stood on the bank.

After throwing a line to Brian so he could anchor it to a large rock beside him, O'Rourke jumped into the shallow water, then climbed up the dirt embankment. When he reached Brian, the captain thrust a cloth bag into his hands. "I thought you might be hungry."

Brian opened the drawstring and peered down at a chunk of brown bread, some cheese, and a link of smoked sausage. His stomach gave a loud rumble.

"It sounds as if I'm just in time." O'Rourke chuckled and clapped him on the shoulder.

Brian nodded, his mouth already filled with the wonderful food. After he finished chewing his first bite, he asked, "What took you so long getting back?"

O'Rourke glanced around the swampy area. "I didn't know how long we'd have to wait out here, so I decided to take on provisions in New Orleans before we sailed upriver."

"That was probably a good thing. Etienne Badeau and most of his crew sailed downriver about the time I thought you would be coming upriver. If he'd seen you, that might have given him cause for concern." Brian sank his teeth into the sausage, releasing a burst of tangy flavor.

"We saw a large schooner go by while we loaded the provisions. I wondered if it was his, but the ship wasn't flying a pirate flag." O'Rourke slapped at his neck.

Brian knew the insects were bothersome in this place. The bites he'd sustained were as aggravating as his other aches and pains. "When we came here, I heard some of the sailors talking about lowering the skull and crossbones before we entered the mouth of the Mississippi. Evidently he got word of a ship carrying a fortune, and he couldn't pass up the chance for it to be his."

"I thought you said he wanted to stop his piracy and settle down on the plantation."

Brian shook his head. "Who knows what the man will do? He's a lunatic." He took another bite of the spicy meat. "He only left six men at the house. At night, two of them stand watch, but evidently they don't think anyone can find the place, because they aren't careful at all. I sneaked onto the balcony and talked to Angelina. I would have helped her escape right then, but her duenna isn't strong enough to get away. So I decided to wait for you to come back."

O'Rourke's gaze took in everything from the bayou to the treetops. "I don't see any plantation house."

"It's up the bayou a ways." Brian gestured toward a narrower part of the waterway, where weeping willows hung out over the water from both sides, their limbs intermingling. "Between those trees."

O'Rourke sat on the big rock where the boat was tied. "What do we do now?"

"I'd like to capture the pirates, but I'm afraid we'd have a hard time controlling them. When Señor Fuente contacted the governor, I'm sure he sent some of his men to help us. They can arrest the pirates and take them to the capital for trial."

"I heard word on the docks that a government ship was expected in New Orleans in a day or two."

Brian took the last bite of the nourishing food, finally feeling satiated. "Maybe we should send someone back to New Orleans in the fishing boat to bring them here. We could move this ship a little farther up the river to another cove. There's less risk of one of the pirates seeing it there. If any of them go to New Orleans to drink, their boat will have to come through this part of the bayou."

O'Rourke stood. "With so few men there, don't you think they'll stay and guard the women?"

"I don't want to take any chances." Brian handed the empty sack to the captain.

The two men got in the boat, and Murphy rowed it to where the merchant ship was anchored. Murphy and a seaman named Godwin took the largest dinghy downriver, riding the current to help them get to New Orleans faster. Brian showed O'Rourke the cove where the ship would be safer from detection by the pirates.

O'Rourke left a skeleton crew on the boat. The rest of the men accompanied him and Brian through the wilderness that surrounded the plantation house. Each man had a small cloth bag with provisions for the day and a flask of fresh water taken from the barrels on board. By midmorning, fifteen men were hidden in the wooded area surrounding the mansion.

Brian chose to be on the side closest to Angelina's room. He hoped to catch a glimpse of her. Just seeing her would settle his mind.

&

When Angelina awakened, her first thoughts were of Brian O'Doule. Where was he right now? How soon would she see him again? If he had been captured, she would have heard something. After he left last night, she wasn't able to go to sleep. She could still feel his arms around her. His masculine smell haunted her, making her long to catch a whiff of it again. He smelled of open air and honest sweat. Her fingers still tingled from the rock hardness of his muscular chest.

Shortly after midnight, Angelina had gone out on the balcony. She had studied the shadowy trees across the lawn from the house, wondering if Brian could be in one of them. Had her father's men returned? Were they waiting until daylight to capture the pirates? Knowing that help was within reach was even worse than waiting for Brian to return.

Because of her late-night excursion on the balcony, Angelina had slept late. When Walter knocked, bringing their breakfast, Angelina was so filled with jubilation over Brian's visit that she didn't think she could hide her joy from the Englishman. She kept quiet, hoping he would think she and her aunt were still asleep. Surely he would bring the food back later.

Angelina threw on her wrapper and walked into the parlor, surprised that Elena wasn't already up. She knocked on her aunt's door, but no answer came. She pushed the door open far enough to peer around it. Her companion was still in bed. Was she sick? Or was something worse wrong? Angelina's heart raced.

When she tiptoed closer, she saw the gentle rise and fall of her aunt's nightgown over her chest, so she was breathing. Angelina started to leave the room but decided to check to see if Aunt Elena had a fever. When Angelina laid her palm against her aunt's brow, it felt cool, so she backed toward the door, trying not to make any sound. Before she reached it, Aunt Elena stirred.

"Angelina?" The frail woman's voice sounded thready.

"Yes." She returned to her aunt's side.

"I'm sorry I slept late." Aunt Elena laid the back of her arm over her eyes. "I've been so tired lately."

Angelina smiled. "It's all right. I didn't get up early, either.

I was awake late into the night."

Aunt Elena scooted up in the bed and rested her back against the headboard. "Are you worried about the pirate being gone?"

Angelina leaned against the side of the bed and crossed her arms. "Actually, I'm excited. Brian came back last night."

Her aunt gasped.

"He sneaked onto the balcony and talked to me."

"Where is he now? Can I see him?" Aunt Elena's color returned and her eyes sparkled with life.

"Brian has seen my father, and he sent some of his men to help. Brian is waiting for them to come up the river. They could be here today."

Aunt Elena turned to climb out of the bed. "We must get dressed so we'll be ready for them."

Angelina took her hand. "We don't know when they will rescue us, and we must keep their presence here a secret. So we can't let Walter guess that we know anything."

"Where is Walter? Why didn't he bring us breakfast?" Aunt Elena asked, walking toward her dressing room.

Angelina laughed at the change in her aunt. "He did, but I didn't answer his knock. I'm sure he thought we were still asleep. He'll probably bring it again soon."

Both women were seated in the parlor by the time Walter brought their breakfast for the second time. Aunt Elena opened the door. She sniffed appreciatively at the appetizing smell that greeted her. She followed Walter to the table and sat primly on one of the couches.

Angelina looked out the window to hide her smile. Was Brian out there now, watching the house? A shiver of anticipation danced down her spine.

"Thank you, Walter."

Aunt Elena's words brought Angelina's attention back toward the meal. She caught her aunt's smile as the Englishman retreated. The return of her duenna's manners, even though the man couldn't understand what she said, gave Angelina hope. In a most unladylike manner, her duenna started shoveling food into her mouth. After so much time without an appetite, Angelina was glad to see her taking sustenance.

"This is delicious," Aunt Elena said between bites.

Angelina laughed. "We've been eating the same thing for breakfast since we came here."

"But it hasn't tasted this good."

When Walter returned to pick up the dishes, Angelina watched him carefully. Did his eyes look astonished at the absence of leftovers on her aunt's dishes? She had left a few bites in her own bowl to try to ward off his suspicions. He glanced at Angelina, and she feigned an expression of indifference.

As soon as Walter shut the door, she breathed a prayer. *Oh, Father God, please keep Walter from noticing anything.*

fourteen

After midnight, while the pirate guards snoozed at their posts, Brian made his way to each of his men stationed in the woods. He told half of them to return to the cove where the ship was anchored. They would sleep for four hours, then take the place of the other men. Brian accompanied the first group to the *St. Augustine*. It felt good to stretch out on the bunk in his cabin. He slept for several hours before Captain O'Rourke knocked on his door to awaken him. Morning sun streamed in through the porthole.

"The ship with the governor's men is coming up the river," O'Rourke announced, the excitement in his voice vibrating throughout the room.

After the captain left, Brian washed up and put on clean clothes. By the time he reached the deck, the other boat had dropped anchor in the murky water of the bayou. A sailor rowed the captain of the governor's guard to the *St. Augustine*. Brian greeted the governor's man and accompanied him to O'Rourke's cabin.

"Captain Herrera, this is Captain O'Rourke." After the two men shook hands, Brian offered the newcomer a straight-backed chair and took a matching one. "So, what are we going to do now?"

Herrera turned his attention from Brian to Captain O'Rourke. "Governor Garrido wants us to capture Etienne Badeau. If we can get him, it should destroy this gang of pirates and make ocean travel safer. Señor Garrido looks forward to having a public trial and execution in St. Augustine. He wants to use it as a warning to any other pirates who might be lurking around this colony."

Brian took measure of the man seated before him. He appeared to be a seasoned soldier who knew what he was talking about. "I believe we can capture most or all of the pirates without endangering the women. Badeau wants to marry Angelina, so he has been kind to her and her aunt, except for keeping them prisoner." Brian propped his forearms on his knees. "Angelina overheard Badeau telling one of his men that he'd heard about a ship carrying a lucrative bounty, so he took off to capture it."

Herrera nodded. "I heard about that ship, too. But just as we sailed away from St. Augustine, it was about to dock there to unload its cargo. If Badeau left only a few days ago, he's too late."

A mirthless laugh exploded from Brian. "Serves him right."

O'Rourke stood and leaned one elbow on the top of a chest. "If that's true, he could be back anytime."

Herrera stood and paced across the small cabin with his hands behind his back. "I don't want to try to catch Badeau on the water. His ship is too fast." He turned and looked at the other two men. "Do you think we can capture the pirates after they're off the ship but before they reach the house?"

O'Rourke smiled. "Etienne Badeau doesn't seem to think anyone can find this remote plantation. So he isn't as careful as he should be. If we want to capture most of the pirates, it might be prudent to wait until they are all together at the house. With our men and your forces, we outnumber them.

Besides, we'll have surprise in our favor."

The three men worked out a plan to keep watch on the river and the plantation house around the clock until the pirate ship returned.

Water lapped against the hull of the ship, rocking it gently. The sound helped calm Brian's nerves. "I'll slip into the plantation house tonight and tell the women what we're doing. When Badeau and his men return, I will go there to protect Angelina and her aunt."

Brian left the ship and went back to his position overlooking the balcony outside Angelina's room. He didn't see her during the heat of the day, but when a fresh breeze blew through the treetops, causing them to dance in the waning light of evening, the curtains parted, and she stepped onto the balcony. She turned her face to catch the cooler air.

Brian feasted his eyes on her beauty, longing for what he knew would never happen.

Angelina wore her hair unbound, hanging freely down her back in waves that rippled in the wind. Light from the room behind her highlighted the ebony curls with a golden halo. She wore a summer dress of some lightweight material that billowed in the wind. Her loveliness made him ache for what he couldn't have, and he knew her beauty wasn't only on the surface. Her heart was pure, and her spirit sweet.

Father God, I love her so much.

20

The weather was hotter than at any time since they had arrived in Spanish West Florida. Angelina wondered how people got used to the oppressive, heavy air that didn't circulate during the hottest part of the day. She wore the coolest dress she owned, and still it clung to her, making her swelter. No wonder this part of the territory was thinly populated. How could people live this way? She had pulled her hair up on top of her head and anchored it into a haphazard bun. After spending the day languishing in the heat, she welcomed the breeze that accompanied the falling of the evening shadows.

Angelina released her hair and stepped out on the balcony, turning her face to catch the wind. It blew her skirt, fanning it and cooling her whole body. She looked around the clearing toward the woods beyond, wondering if Brian was out there. She felt as if she were connected to him as he watched over her and her aunt. Angelina remembered the feel of his strength as he held her against his chest. She had heard his heartbeat accelerate as hers had done. When they escaped from this place, a relationship with Brian O'Doule would be her goal. Of course, she didn't know what her father would think about that, but maybe he would be so glad to have her safely home that he would want to make her happy. She hoped so.

Aunt Elena slipped between the curtains and joined her on the balcony. "It's cooler out here, isn't it?" Her aunt stood with her arms crossed over her waist and gazed into the distance. "This could be a pleasant place if it didn't belong to that awful man."

"And if it weren't so hot."

Her duenna leaned both arms on the railing. "I imagine it's cooler on the first floor, and even more so in the basement. If we were free to move around the house, it would be quite livable. It's too bad some nice family can't own this wonderful property."

After Aunt Elena went back into the parlor, Angelina dropped into the chair she kept on the balcony. She picked up Brian's Bible and held it close to her heart, running her fingers over the texture of the leather. She listened to her aunt's footsteps as she approached her bedroom. The snap of the door latch followed. Her companion usually went to bed at this time, but Angelina couldn't sleep, wondering what was going on out there in the woods around the plantation house.

Soon after the lamplight in her duenna's room was extinguished, the branches of the tree near the balcony rustled. Angelina's gaze probed the darkness, trying to make out a shape. Was she imagining that she saw Brian? Did she want him with her so much that she saw him in every shadow?

When his feet dropped below the level of the lower branch, Angelina's heart leaped with joy. She stood, laid the Bible in the chair, and watched his sinewy body lower gracefully to the floor beside her, his feet making a soft thud when they landed.

A smile lit his face. "Angelina." Her name sounded like music on his tongue, and a melting sensation started inside her.

"Brian." She returned his smile. "I wondered if you would come again tonight."

He stepped closer, and the heat from his body radiated toward her, yet he didn't touch her. "You need to know what's happening."

Angelina wanted to throw herself into his arms, but he seemed to be holding back. She didn't want him to think her wanton. She clasped her hands at her waist to keep them from trembling.

❧

Brian wanted to gather Angelina into his arms, but how could he? He had already held her more times than any man should who wasn't going to be her husband. A capricious breeze picked up a lock of her hair and blew it across her face. He longed to reach over and push it behind her delicate ear. She stood too close for comfort, so he took a step backward and looked out over the lawn bathed in moonlight.

"Governor Carlos Garrido's men arrived today." He took a deep breath and turned back to face her. "We're going to keep the house under surveillance until Badeau returns. Garrido wants all the pirates captured. We don't want the guards here to suspect anything's wrong, so we're going to wait for his return before making a move. If his men aren't in plain sight when he arrives, Badeau might make a run for it before we can catch him. And there's no way we could take you away without his men finding out. Will you be all right until then?"

Angelina's gaze bore into his, burning with an expression he wished he could understand. "I agree. Etienne Badeau must be captured." She spat the name as if it tasted bitter in her mouth. "Aunt Elena and I will do whatever you think best."

Brian took a step toward her. "I promise I won't let any harm come to you."

№

No one had to tell Brian that Badeau had returned. The man's angry bellows echoed through the woods surrounding the plantation house. Brian made his way as close to the cove as he dared and watched the pirates disembark from their schooner.

Brian observed the pirates unload wooden crates and haul them up the bayou. The last boat to leave the pirate ship held Badeau and Miles Henderson, his first mate, along with a sailor who rowed the dinghy.

Brian worked his way through the underbrush as fast as he could without alerting anyone to his presence. He wanted to be near the house when Badeau arrived.

Walter waited for the other two pirates in front of the house. "Etienne, why were you bellowing like a wounded bear?"

The giant stomped the rest of the way up the hill. "We were too late to intercept the ship. This was a wasted trip."

The Englishman almost cringed before he straightened and spoke again. "The treasure room is full. Even after you pay all the men their shares, you'll be a very wealthy man."

Badeau glared at Walter. "And what good will that do me?" The tall pirate gestured toward the upper story of the house. "I still can't communicate with the woman. How can I encourage her to be my wife if we can't talk to each other?"

Walter turned toward the house, and Brian saw the smile he hid from his boss. "Maybe you'll have to capture someone else who speaks both French and Spanish."

Badeau stood with his feet planted apart and his hands on his hips. "I wouldn't need to if you hadn't let the gators have the other one for supper."

Brian glanced toward where Captain Herrera watched everything that was happening. Captain O'Rourke was on the other side of the house, and all their men were spread out on the perimeter of the clearing, waiting for a signal.

Brian stepped from his cover. "Badeau!" At his shouted word, the pirate turned and glared at him. "I'm too tough. The alligators didn't want me."

With an animal-like roar, Badeau charged across the clearing, drawing his sword as he came toward Brian. "They'll make a meal out of you when I get through carving you into tiny pieces."

Brian felt a momentary fear but dismissed it quickly. "I don't think so."

His calm demeanor caused the pirate to stop abruptly. "Why not?"

As if in answer to the pirate's question, other men stepped out of the cover of the underbrush. Some brandished swords; others a pistol, flintlock, or blunderbuss. The pirate captain looked around, rage covering his face. Another animal sound exploded from him, and he lunged toward Brian, thrusting his sword at him.

Anticipating Badeau's move, Brian sprinted toward the side of the house. The pirate lumbered after him. The blast of guns and the smell of burnt gunpowder filled the air. When the pirate captain yelled in pain, Brian glanced over his shoulder. Badeau grabbed his thigh, and blood ran between his fingers. He plunged to the ground but quickly sat up, holding his sword ready to slash at anyone who ventured near. Pirates poured from the house. Just as quickly, the governor's guards and Señor Fuente's men came out of hiding. The clash of steel on steel accompanied the sound of gunfire all around the clearing.

Brian shimmied up the tree and dropped onto the balcony outside Angelina's room. He crouched behind the railing and studied the scene below. A full-fledged battle took place on the lawn, but the governor's guard had the upper hand. When he heard the door open behind him, Brian turned around. He jumped up and pushed Angelina back inside, away from the windows, shielding her with his body as he held her close to his chest.

"I'm sorry. But you don't want to be hit by a stray bullet."

An exclamation from Elena caught Brian's attention. He looked at her and opened one arm. The older woman quickly moved toward him, and he gathered her close, as well.

"Father God, please protect us from any harm. Help the men outside capture the pirates quickly."

Brian continued to hold the women and pray for what felt like an eternity. Finally, the melee outside quieted down.

"Angelina, Elena, please wait here." Brian ushered them toward the nearest settee. "I'll come get you when it's safe."

As Brian stepped out on the balcony, the men under his command were corralling most of the pirates, while the governor's guard tied them up with ropes that Captain Herrera had brought with him.

"Good job," he shouted down to them.

Captain O'Rourke turned from where he stood close to the house. "Are the women all right?"

"They're fine." Brian looked at the pirates. "Is that all of them?"

Herrera nodded. "When the fighting began, a few turned tail and ran. I don't think many escaped. But the ones who did can tell any other brigands they meet just what happens to pirates in Spanish West Florida."

Brian looked around for Walter. Finally, he saw him tied to Etienne Badeau. "That man with Badeau." He pointed toward the Englishman. "He has all the keys to the rooms."

Herrera hurried over to Walter and removed the large ring of skeleton keys from Walter's belt.

Brian waved to him. "Please bring them up and unlock the women's door."

fifteen

After O'Rourke unlocked the door that connected the parlor with the hallway, he gave the keys to Brian. "Ladies." He tipped his hat before retreating through the open doorway.

Angelina couldn't think of a thing to say. They weren't prisoners anymore. She was relieved that the door was no longer locked, but they were still in the wilderness of Spanish West Florida, away from civilization. She looked at Brian. "What happens now?"

"What would you like to do?" he asked.

"I want to look at the house." Angelina gazed up at him. "When we went through it with Badeau, I was so upset I didn't really pay attention."

Brian led them from room to room. The house was large and airy, with areas that utilized many windows to let in the light. When they finished examining all the bedrooms on the second floor, they went downstairs. Aunt Elena was right—it did feel much cooler down there. They went into a music room complete with a pianoforte, its carved square case polished and shining in the sunlight. It was beautiful, but Angelina wondered if Etienne Badeau had stolen that, too. Surely none of the pirates could play this beautiful instrument. She certainly hadn't heard it while they were in the house.

Elena smiled at her niece. "Why don't you show us what this sounds like?" She turned toward Brian. "Angelina took lessons on the pianoforte while she was in Spain. She became quite accomplished at it."

Angelina touched one ivory key, and the tinkle the instrument emitted was a strange contrast to the sounds of the swamp coming through the open windows. At least now she, her aunt, and Brian were on the back of the house, where the harsh disagreements between the soldiers and pirates didn't intrude.

After sliding onto the stool in front of the pianoforte, Angelina ran through some scales, then played a lilting melody. When she finished and clasped her hands in her lap, applause filled the room.

Brian then led the women to the kitchen, which sat a little ways behind the main structure, connected by a covered walkway. "It was built over there to keep from heating the house in summer."

A fire burned in the fireplace, and a tempting aroma wafted from the pot hanging over the flames. Evidently the cook had rushed out when he heard the uproar. Aunt Elena went over and stirred the stew with a wooden spoon she found hanging on the wall nearby. She swung the kettle away from the flames so the food wouldn't be ruined by overcooking.

They returned to the house, and as they entered the foyer, the front door opened. Captain Herrera and Captain O'Rourke came inside. Herrera smiled at the trio. "We need to talk."

Brian led the way into the parlor. After they all sat, he looked at the captain of the governor's guards. "So, what happens now?"

The man rubbed his forehead as if to stave off a headache.

"We've sent some of the sailors to bring both of the other ships to the cove where the schooner is anchored. I'm going to load all the pirates onto my ship. We can lock them in the holds. Several of the compartments have shackles for the most uncooperative."

Brian nodded. "That sounds good."

"I'm going to leave a few of my men here to guard the plantation house. If any of the pirates who escaped during the battle come back, we'll capture them, too."

"What about all the treasure in the basement?" Brian asked with a frown. "There is a lot of loot in there. Part of it came from the *Angelina Star*."

"The pirate captain brought me gifts." Angelina grimaced. "I'm sure many of them came from that treasure cache. I'd like for them all to go back to their rightful owners. I didn't use any of them. I. . .I just couldn't."

Captain Herrera rubbed the back of his neck. "We'll return everything we can. But you need to pack your belongings. I'll take the key to the treasure room to Governor Garrido, but I'll leave the other keys with the men who stay here."

O'Rourke stood. "Should we take the women back to St. Augustine?"

Herrera studied his hands. "Do you have enough men with you to sail two ships?"

"Yes."

"Good." Herrera turned toward Brian. "You and the women will go on one ship, and your extra men can take the pirate schooner to St. Augustine. We'll leave the small fishing boat for the men at the house. If they run out of supplies before someone returns for them, they can sail to New Orleans for more."

"What about Señor Fuente's merchandise?" When Brian looked at her, Angelina averted her eyes. She didn't want him to see how intently she had been staring at him. "Can we take that from the treasure room?"

Angelina was pleased that Brian was looking out for her father's interests. It showed what a thoughtful man he was. Perhaps if her father got his merchandise back, that would make up in part for losing his favorite ship.

❧

Angelina stepped into the warm bathwater and reached for a bar of the soap made from olive oil and scented with lavender that she had brought with her from Spain. This would be the last time she bathed in the suite of rooms that had been her prison. But she was no longer a prisoner; she was free. It felt better than she remembered.

As she lathered her arms, she couldn't keep her thoughts from drifting to Brian. After Captain Herrera sailed away, Brian suggested that the other two ships wait until the next morning to leave. This allowed time for Angelina and her aunt to wash their clothes and hang them outside to dry, so they would be clean when Angelina and her aunt packed their trunks.

Brian had stayed close to the women the rest of the day. The memory of his smile, often turned toward her, caused Angelina's heart to skip a beat. His laughing eyes were the same color as the summer sky that showed in patches between the tree limbs surrounding the house. Now that they were no longer prisoners, he had a carefree air about him, making her love him even more. His voice sent chills down her spine in a most delicious way. The shiny waves of his dark hair blew in the wind and danced around his head. Earlier in the day, he had shaved off the beard he had worn since returning to rescue her. She was glad she could see all of his face now. Why hadn't she ever noticed how handsome he was during all the years he worked for her father? Probably because she was a girl when she went to visit her grandparents, but now she was a woman. A woman in love with Brian O'Doule.

"Are you about through, mi ángel?" Aunt Elena's voice from the other side of the door brought her out of her reverie.

"Almost." She splashed water over her back to rinse off the last of the soap. It felt cool. She must have been dreaming about Brian long enough for the water to turn tepid.

Angelina stood and reached for the towel. "You should ask Brian to bring up some more hot water, or you will have a cold bath." After she finished drying off and putting on her clean clothes, she opened the dressing room door. "Is the hot water here yet?"

"No." Her duenna entered, carrying her toiletries. "But it has been so hot today, I won't mind a cool bath."

❧

Brian stood on the balcony of his bedroom. He had chosen a room at the opposite end from the women's quarters, because he didn't want to be tempted by knowing Angelina was next door. Tomorrow they would leave this place. If they had arrived under different circumstances, he would have enjoyed the time they spent here. Being with Angelina was the best thing that had ever happened in his life. Today had been particularly special, as he watched every graceful move she made. Her smile spoke straight to his heart.

Elena seemed more relaxed, too. She hadn't kept such a sharp eye on their activities, as if she knew they needed time to relax together. After the clothes were washed, he and

Angelina walked all around the large clearing, talking about everything and nothing. However was he going to live so close to her in St. Augustine and not be a part of her life? Since he couldn't have any future with her, maybe it was time to move on. He had settled in St. Augustine, hoping to spend the rest of his life there. But he couldn't watch Angelina fall in love with someone else or even have a husband chosen for her by her father. It would break Brian's heart to watch that wedding take place. Just thinking about it hurt so much.

Father God, help me know what to do.

Brian spent an uneasy night poring over the Bible Angelina had returned to him the evening before. With the coming of dawn, peace finally descended on his heart. He felt an assurance that the Lord would help him face whatever was to come.

He and O'Rourke decided to load the merchandise on the merchant ship and take the women on the faster pirate schooner. It had been a difficult decision because of the memories associated with the vessel, but they wanted to return Angelina to her father as quickly as they could. After the men took everything out of the captain's quarters and washed it down, hopefully the women could think of it as only a cabin on a ship. At least on this voyage, they wouldn't be prisoners.

That afternoon, they stopped in New Orleans to take on supplies, then made their way to the delta of the Mississippi River. Having the current in their favor would make the ship move faster. As they sailed out into the Gulf of Mexico, the setting sun painted a blinding path across indigo waters. Angelina and Elena stood beside Brian and O'Rourke on the quarterdeck.

"It is so nice to be able to leave the cabin and feel freedom,"

Elena said. Even she seemed different without the constraints that had controlled their lives for so long. She acted as if she were almost as young as her niece.

O'Rourke smiled at her. When she smiled back at him with a special light in her eyes, Brian wondered if everyone except himself would have a happy ending to this adventure.

"We carefully chose the men who are sailing on this ship." O'Rourke spoke to Elena as if no one else were around. "Of course, your brother-in-law only sent his most trusted men on this mission, so Brian and I felt we didn't have to keep you cut off from everyone else."

"And we warned the men to show you and Angelina utmost respect," Brian added.

O'Rourke and Elena sat on a bench attached to the wall, and Brian leaned against the railing beside Angelina, watching the last sliver of sun slip below the horizon. While the two older people were deep in conversation, the twinkle of stars ushered in the evening breeze, which filled the sails to capacity, skimming the ship over the waves at a fast clip.

Angelina turned to look up at him, her eyes sparkling as brightly as the stars. "I was worried when you took so long to return." Her husky words were a whisper for his ears alone. "When Etienne Badeau said you'd probably been eaten by the alligators, my heart almost broke."

Brian didn't know what to say. Had she meant what it sounded like she said? Would her heart break to lose him?

"I was glad you left your Bible in our room. I read it every day because I wanted the same kind of relationship with God that you have. I asked Jesus into my life, and He gave me the assurance that you were not dead. I held on to that hope as a lifeline." Tears glistened on her dark lashes.

Brian brushed them away with his thumb. "I would never have left without returning for you." His eyes dropped to her trembling lips, a pale rose shade in the moonlight. He knew he couldn't do what he wanted to right then, so he turned and looked at the pathway of light that spread from the ship to the horizon in the direction of the moon, which hung low in the sky.

"I knew you wouldn't." Angelina put her gentle hand on his arm. "Thank you."

He needed to be truthful with her. She shouldn't think of him as some kind of hero. If it hadn't been for him, they wouldn't have been captured. He knew that when he told her the truth, her feelings for him would likely change, but he had to do it anyway.

"Angelina. . .I must make a confession to you." The words tasted hard on his tongue.

Grasping the railing with both hands, she turned her face up to him, and he imprinted every feature of her smile in his memory.

"I was in the crow's nest that day." How much should he tell her?

"I know. I saw you up there."

"But I wasn't keeping watch as closely as I should have been." The words ripped his heart. "It's my fault we were captured."

Angelina gasped. "Oh, Brian, how can you think that?"

"If I'd been watching, we would have seen the pirate ship sooner and might have had a chance to outrun them."

"With the heavy load of merchandise in the holds of the *Angelina Star*, don't you think the pirate ship would have been able to overtake her no matter when we saw them?"

Brian mulled over that thought. "I suppose so. You know I

would never put anyone in danger if I could help it."

Angelina looked at the moon's path on the water. She was quiet for a few moments before she spoke. "Brian, what distracted you so much? Was it the birds flying overhead? We hadn't seen any over the middle of the ocean."

She was smart as well as beautiful. Brian wanted to agree with her and put the blame on the gulls that dipped and soared above the ship that day. But he hadn't lied to her before, and he wasn't going to start now, even if it meant she would never speak to him again.

"From the crow's nest, I could see you clearly behind the sail curtain. Your beauty was so breathtaking, I couldn't take my eyes off you." When he looked down at her, he saw the blush that stained her cheeks in the moonlight.

She turned her gaze back to his face, letting her eyes roam over every feature. Brian felt as if she were caressing him with her eyes. "Then I'm as much at fault as you are."

Heedless of anyone else who might see him, he grasped her shoulders with both hands. "You did nothing wrong, so it couldn't be your fault."

Her laugh sounded like a tinkling bell. "I knew you were looking at me, and I liked it. Although I didn't look directly at you, I watched you out of the corner of my eye. I saw the expression on your face when I spread my arms to the wind." She gazed into the depths of his eyes. "Do you think me a wanton woman for preening before you?"

Brian wanted to gather her into his arms and nestle her head against his chest. He wanted to hold her there for an eternity, covering her face with his kisses. If only they were alone. . .If only they didn't have an audience. . .If only it were his right.

Angelina wanted Brian to kiss her more than she had wanted anything else in her life. How could she ever live without him? She didn't even want to think of a future with no Brian O'Doule in it.

"Angelina." Her name rolled off his tongue like music. "I wish I were the kind of man your father would want for your husband."

She stepped closer to him. "But what if I want you for my husband?"

"Without his permission, it wouldn't be right." His face clouded with sorrow.

"Brian, do you love me?" She had to hear him say the words, at least once.

With a groan, he pulled her into his arms. She could hear his heart beating in time with hers. It thundered at a fast pace, so she placed her hand over his muscles, loving the feel of his pulse.

"How can you ask me that, Angelina? I have no right to declare my affections for you."

She kept her head against his chest, not daring to look into his face. "What if I give you the right?"

"Oh, Angelina, if I tell you that I love you and your father does not allow us to marry, won't it hurt that much more?"

She felt his head drop against the top of hers, his breath disturbing her curls. "It would hurt even more to never have heard you say the words." She didn't think he could hear her whisper.

He must have, because he took a deep breath, then exhaled. "Angelina, I love you with all my heart. If your father won't allow us to marry, my life will be over."

She grasped the front of his shirt with trembling hands, eling as if she might swoon. "And I love you, Brian."

He gently kissed the top of her head, then laid his cheek ainst the spot. She stood reveling in the feel of his arms d the spicy masculine scent that wafted around her until unt Elena called her to go to the cabin.

sixteen

Brian stood on deck before dawn. The prevailing wind had been in their favor on the whole trip across the Gulf of Mexico and up the eastern coastline of the Florida peninsula. The schooner made excellent time. Maybe too good. He and Angelina had spent every waking minute together. . .under the watchful eyes of Elena.

Today they might reach the port of St. Augustine. His idyllic time would soon end, and reality would intrude. Brian gazed toward the east, where the sun, barely below the horizon, painted the few clouds drifting on the ocean breeze with soft shades of pinks and purples against the brightening blue sky. He couldn't watch the beauty of a sunrise without thanking God for His handiwork, but deep inside a lump of fear lurked, feeling almost like an anchor keeping his heart from taking wings with praise. Even though he and Angelina had pledged their love to each other more than once on the voyage, he knew that being a man of honor would keep him from going against the expressed wishes of her father if he was against the union. Would Señor Fuente stand in the way of their happiness?

"Brian." Angelina's gentle voice called from behind him. "What are you doing on deck so early?"

He turned, and the emerging sun bathed her in a golden light, making her look more like a heavenly angel than ever. His breath whooshed out in a painful rush. Her lovely smile pierced his heart. "I'm watching the sunrise."

Angelina walked closer, and the faint aroma of lavender invaded his senses. "Don't let me stop you. It is especially beautiful this morning."

Without taking his eyes from her, he said, "Yes, it is." He turned back to lean on the railing beside her, facing the ocean.

"I like you without your beard." Angelina touched his cheek with the fingertips of one hand.

Her touch was exquisite torture. He enclosed her fingers in his hand and pulled it down before releasing his hold. "If we keep up this pace, we should reach St. Augustine sometime this morning."

She turned to grasp the top railing with both hands. "I'm eager to see my father. . .but I don't want our time together to end."

The last words came out in a whisper. Brian had to lean closer to Angelina to catch them. "We must trust God to take care of everything for us." He stated the words with more conviction than he felt.

"Angelina," Elena's voice called from the open doorway. "It's time to break our fast."

★

When they sailed into the harbor at St. Augustine, Angelina stood with Aunt Elena on the quarterdeck. The governor's ship carrying the pirate captives was already docked at the first wharf. Angelina found her father at once, standing at the end of the second wharf. He shaded his eyes against the rays of the sun glaring down from almost straight above.

"There he is!" she shouted. She frantically waved one arm and continued until he returned the greeting. She grabbed her duenna and started dancing around the deck.

Aunt Elena pulled on Angelina's arms to calm her. "Do you want him to think you're still the child who left here a year and a half ago? Or do you want him to see the woman you have become?"

Those questions sobered Angelina. Yes, she wanted him to see her as a woman. A woman who was mature enough to know what she wanted. A woman old enough to marry Brian O'Doule. She stood still and straightened her clothing, which was in disarray from her exuberant display. Inside, she might be the girl who could hardly wait to hug her father, but on the outside, she wanted him to recognize the differences in her.

By the time they were tied up with the gangplank lowered, Angelina had composed herself. Accompanied by Captain O'Rourke and Brian, she and her aunt disembarked. When her feet were solidly planted on the rough boards of the wharf, her father stood beside her.

"My Angelina." Although he had never been very demonstrative in public, he pulled her into his arms.

She looked up into his face, noticing the trails of tears down his wrinkled cheeks. She threw her arms around his neck and hugged him back. "I've missed you, Papá."

He continued to hold her even though people worked around them on the busy waterfront. "I missed you, too. More than you can know," he whispered. "When I thought you were dead, I felt like giving up." The last word caught on a sob.

Angelina leaned back in his embrace and bracketed his face with her palms. "Oh, Papá, don't think about that now. I'm home, alive and well."

"Yes, you are." He kissed her cheek, then stepped back and took her arm. "Come. I'm sure Bridgett has a feast waiting for you and Elena."

Angelina started to say something, but her aunt intervened. "What about Captain O'Rourke and Brian O'Doule? After all, they rescued us."

"Of course, they're welcome, too." Her father turned and invited the two men to accompany them in the shiny black coach that waited on the cobbled street nearby.

❧

The meal was a celebration accompanied by laughter and happy conversation. Afterward, Señor Fuente invited the four of them to retire to the parlor with him. Captain O'Rourke thanked his host for his hospitality but said he wanted to make sure the women's luggage would be brought to the house as soon as possible.

The sitting room windows had been opened to welcome the ocean breezes. Brian looked out toward the bustling shoreline. "It's amazing how different the weather is here from that in Spanish West Florida." He turned back toward the others. "The wind off the ocean keeps this house cool. There the summer is hot and muggy. Only the lower floors of the plantation home offered relief in the middle of the day."

His employer gestured toward a nearby chair. "Brian, please make yourself comfortable."

He rested on the cushioned seat of the straight-backed chair, and Angelina sat on the divan beside her duenna. Once again he felt like just an employee. His heart ached for more.

"You were gone a lot longer than I thought you would be." Señor Fuente's expression didn't hold censure, just curiosity.

"I have much to tell you." Brian crossed one leg over the other and stuffed his hands in the front pockets of his trousers. He hoped his employer couldn't tell how nervous he was.

"Captain Herrera told me most of what happened. At first, I wasn't very happy about you men leaving my daughter and her companion in that house so long, but he explained that Governor Garrido didn't want to take a chance on Badeau or any of his underlings getting away. And you believed the women were safe. I'm glad you were right."

Brian cleared his throat. "I would never have agreed if I thought anyone would hurt them. You can be assured of that."

Señor Fuente nodded. "I'm not upbraiding you." He rubbed his hands down his thighs. "I'm thankful for all you've done for us."

An uneasy silence descended on the room. Angelina finally broke it. "Papá, Brian was very brave. He kept close watch over Aunt Elena and me. We were never in any real danger."

Señor Fuente smiled indulgently at his daughter. "I'm sure you're right."

Elena raised an eyebrow at her brother-in-law. "Perhaps I could go up to my room. I'd like to rest a few minutes before I'll need to unpack."

"Of course." Señor Fuente stood and clasped her hand to help her up. He turned toward his daughter. "Do you need to rest, too?"

She smiled up at him. "No, Papá. I'll stay here with you."

After Elena stepped through the doorway, he sat on the settee beside Angelina and turned to Brian. "Perhaps we should discuss what we talked about before you went to rescue my daughter. I often thought about it while you were gone."

"Sir?" Brian wasn't sure what part of their conversation the man was referring to.

"You said you were distracted in the crow's nest. Brian, that doesn't sound like you. You've always been very diligent, no matter what your task. I've been trying to figure out what on that ship could have distracted you so much. Weren't you in the middle of the ocean with no land in sight?"

Here it comes, Lord. Am I going to have to confess everything to him right now? Brian's silent prayer didn't calm his nerves. "Yes, sir. The only thing around was the ship and gulls flying overhead."

"And gulls distracted you?" His employer's expression told Brian he found that unbelievable.

"No, sir. It wasn't the gulls, although I did enjoy watching them." Brian could feel heat flood his face. "I knew their presence meant we weren't too far from shore." He gulped.

"I'm afraid I was partly to blame." At the sound of her voice, both men turned their attention to Angelina. "I was out on deck that day with Aunt Elena."

Her father took her hand in his. "Didn't the captain place a privacy curtain to protect you from the eyes of the crew?"

"Yes." Angelina looked up at her father sitting beside her.

"But I was in the crow's nest, sir. And I could see behind the curtain."

Brian had just finished his sentence when Angelina added, "I knew he was up there watching, and I moved to stand by the railing so I could be in plain sight."

Señor Fuente frowned at Brian. "You were distracted by my daughter?"

"I know there's no excuse for it." Brian placed both feet on the floor and clasped his hands in front of his waist. "I've felt a great amount of guilt over allowing us to be overtaken by the pirates. I hold myself completely responsible, and I know I can never make it up to you for losing your favorite ship or allowing Angelina to fall into the clutches of that brigand." Brian hung his head.

His employer stood and walked to the window to stare toward the ocean in the distance. "Captain Herrera told me that the pirate schooner is a very fast sailing ship. And the *Angelina Star* had every hold loaded down with cargo. There is probably no way she could have outrun the other vessel. I don't hold you responsible in any way."

Brian glanced at Angelina. Her smile lit his heart.

Señor Fuente turned his back on the window. "Do we need to discuss my daughter? I saw the way the two of you looked at each other during supper."

Brian stood and crossed the room. "I did want to talk to you about her. I thought I would wait until we were alone."

"Angelina, go to your room." Brian was surprised by his employer's words and the tone of his voice.

She must have been, too. Angelina stood and stared defiantly at her father. "No. I am no longer a child. I want to hear what the two of you have to say about me."

Señor Fuente nodded. "I thought you would." When he smiled at his daughter, she relaxed and gave him a hug. He turned to Brian. "Now, what did you want to talk about?"

Once again, Brian stuffed his hands into his front pockets. It seemed to be the only way he could hold them steady. "Well, sir. . .I love Angelina, and I would like to marry her. But I won't do anything without your permission."

Señor Fuente frowned. "You didn't have my permission to fall in love with her."

This wasn't going very well. Brian cleared his throat. "I know, but I couldn't not love her, sir." Had that statement made any sense?

"And I love Brian, Father." Brian noticed that she didn't use the pet name she had always called her Papá. He wondered if Señor Fuente did, too. "I've seen him in bad circumstances and good, and he always did everything he could to protect Aunt Elena and me. He made our imprisonment bearable. . .even pleasant sometimes."

Arturo Fuente gave his daughter a piercing gaze. "Could what you feel be a special affection brought on by the fact that he rescued you? That would make you extremely grateful."

Angelina shook her head. "No, Papá."

The older man cleared his throat. "Did he take advantage of you or the situation?"

"Papá!" Angelina took a step toward her father. "Aunt Elena was a wonderful chaperone. Besides, Brian is a godly man."

Señor Fuente turned to face Brian. "Would you ever dishonor her?"

Brian gave an emphatic shake of his head. "Never! I want to marry her. . .if you will give your permission."

A ringing silence descended on the room. Brian hoped his employer would agree. If he didn't, Brian would have to leave St. Augustine. Maybe he could return to the sea. He had quite a bit of money saved. Señor Fuente had been a generous employer, and his own needs hadn't been more than a roof over his head and food to eat. Maybe he could go somewhere and start over. . .but with a broken heart.

"Is that what you want, my daughter?" Angelina's father moved toward her and took one of her hands in both of his.

"To marry this man?"

She nodded. Brian could see tears glistening on her dark eyelashes. "More than anything else in the world."

"He is not a Catholic." Her father studied her expression.

"But he is a good man. I've gotten to know him very well, and I respect him. I know he will love me with all his heart."

He let go of her hand and turned toward Brian. "I've thought about nothing else but my daughter since I found out she's alive. Since I believed I had lost her to death, I'm thankful to know that isn't true. I'd give her anything she asked for within my means. And I owe you a great debt for saving her and protecting her. In the old country, I never would have given her in marriage to anyone outside the Catholic Church. But we live in a new world. Things are different here. I believe her when she tells me you are a godly man. If you are what she wants, I'll not stand in the way." The man turned to gaze out the windows.

That wasn't good enough for Brian. He didn't want Señor Fuente to just allow it. "Sir, I would like to have your blessing on our marriage. Can you give us that?"

The two men looked at each other for a few moments.

"Yes, you have my blessing." The older man gave his daughter a smile, then left the room.

Brian stared at Angelina. She reached up and wiped her eyes with the backs of her hands. Although her lashes were still wet, no tears threatened to fall. She took one hesitant step toward him. With long strides, he crossed the room and pulled her into his arms.

She rested her head against his chest. "Do you have something to ask me, Brian?"

What was she talking about? Then the fog lifted from his

brain. He loosened his hold on her so she could look up into his eyes.

"Angelina de la Fuente Delgado, would you do me the honor of becoming my wife?"

She lifted a hand and caressed his cheek. "Oh, yes, my love."

Brian had waited a long time for this moment. He slowly lowered his face toward hers. Just before their lips met, her eyes drifted shut. Sweetness poured over him like warm honey. He tasted it on her lips, their softness firming under the pressure from his. *So this is what love tastes like.* Brian wanted the moment to last forever. He pulled back and caught a look of wonder on her face. Once again, his lips descended to hers, gently at first, but increasing in intensity. Her arms crept up around his neck, and her fingers tangled in the waves there. He was glad he hadn't had time to get his hair trimmed. As she twirled curls around her fingers, the gentle tug intensified their connection to each other.

Angelina wound her fingers in the tangled curls on the nape of his neck while his lips pledged his eternal love to her. *We are getting married.* The hoped-for event would come to pass. It was almost too much to imagine. When Brian deepened the kiss, Angelina felt as if she were being transported to the very gates of heaven. That's what life with Brian would be—heaven on earth for her.

epilogue

Three months later

Angelina looked around the table at her wedding dinner. The ceremony had been the event of the year in St. Augustine. Most of the townspeople were customers at Señor Fuente's store, so they went to the church to see the couple exchange their vows. At this meal Bridgett prepared for the family and close friends, Carlos Garrido made two announcements. Because the pirates had destroyed Señor Fuente's favorite ship, the governor gave him ownership of the schooner to replace it.

"Soon after the return of the captives," Señor Garrido said, smiling at Angelina and her aunt, "I accompanied Captain Herrera to the plantation to clean out the treasure room. We will attempt to find the owners of whatever we can, but the rest will become part of the treasury of the colony."

A smattering of applause went round the table, but the governor wasn't finished. "I left several of my men protecting the plantation house. It's a magnificent structure. I believe there could be a real future for anyone who owns that parcel of land. That part of the country is just beginning to grow and develop. Both as a reward for his part in capturing the pirates, and as a wedding present, I am deeding the plantation to Brian O'Doule."

This time the applause was almost deafening. Angelina

looked at Brian. She could tell that the governor's generosity amazed him as much as it did her.

She leaned closer to her new husband. "What do you think about that?"

Brian gazed deep into her eyes. "More important is what you think about it. Could you ever live in that house again?"

Angelina thought about it for a moment. "I can live anywhere with you."

"But do you want to go back?"

She recognized the gleam of hope in his eyes. "Aunt Elena and I often said it was a shame the plantation wasn't home to some family. It would be a good place to establish ours, wouldn't it?"

His smile dazzled her. "Yes." Even though people were watching them, he touched his lips to hers, and everything inside her melted.

Within a week, the schooner sailed from St. Augustine. Papá had made Michael O'Rourke the captain of his new ship. Aunt Elena agreed to move to the plantation with them, and Captain O'Rourke said he might be a frequent visitor between voyages. Perhaps the plantation would soon become the center of social gatherings.

Angelina didn't need a chaperone, but her aunt wanted to serve as her housekeeper. Keeping up with such a large household would take more than one person. They brought another woman to help with the housework and a second woman who would be their cook. They could hire any other help they needed after they arrived at their destination. The holds of the ship contained many of the items Papá had saved for Angelina after her mother died.

Her father promised to come to the plantation by Christmas.

He wanted to find a portrait artist to bring with him so that Angelina could have hers painted in the jewels her grandparents gave her. The red velvet dress her mother wore in the painting in her father's parlor rested in the bottom of one of the trunks. By the time her father and the portrait painter arrived, Angelina would have made the plantation house her own, adding personal touches that gave it her personality and erased any bad memories that might linger. Someday she and Brian would pass the jewels down to their own daughter—if God gave them one.

When at last the schooner anchored in the cove near the house, Brian helped Angelina into the first boat to go ashore. They held hands and strolled on the pathway up the hill. This time everything looked different to Angelina. Without pirates around, the air felt fresher, and every tree and bush welcomed them into the serenity of the bayou country of Spanish West Florida. This was her home now, not her prison. She felt as if God had cleaned all the old feelings of fear and distrust out of her heart and replaced them with His love and the love of her wonderful husband.

"Every plantation deserves a name." Brian stopped and studied the house. "What should we call ours?"

Angelina smiled. "I think Pirate's Prize fits it very well."

Brian laughed, pulled her into his arms, and kissed her until her toes curled and her knees felt weak.

A Letter To Our Readers

Dear Reader:

In order that we might better contribute to your reading enjoyment, we would appreciate your taking a few minutes to respond to the following questions. We welcome your comments and read each form and letter we receive. When completed, please return to the following:

Fiction Editor
Heartsong Presents
PO Box 719
Uhrichsville, Ohio 44683

1. Did you enjoy reading *Pirate's Prize* by Lena Nelson Dooley?
   ❏ Very much! I would like to see more books by this author!
   ❏ Moderately. I would have enjoyed it more if

   _____

   _____

   _____

2. Are you a member of **Heartsong Presents**? ❏ Yes ❏ No
   If no, where did you purchase this book? _____

   _____

3. How would you rate, on a scale from 1 (poor) to 5 (superior), the cover design? _____

4. On a scale from 1 (poor) to 10 (superior), please rate the following elements.

   ____ Heroine   ____ Plot
   ____ Hero   ____ Inspirational theme
   ____ Setting   ____ Secondary characters

5. These characters were special because? _____

_____

_____

6. How has this book inspired your life? _____

_____

_____

7. What settings would you like to see covered in future
   Heartsong Presents books? _____

_____

_____

8. What are some inspirational themes you would like to see
   treated in future books? _____

_____

_____

9. Would you be interested in reading other **Heartsong
   Presents** titles? ❏ Yes   ❏ No

10. Please check your age range:

    ❏ Under 18   ❏ 18-24
    ❏ 25-34   ❏ 35-45
    ❏ 46-55   ❏ Over 55

Name _____

Occupation _____

Address _____

City, State, Zip _____

Texas Dreams

4 stories in 1

As newlyweds in 1853, Daniel and Mary Anna Thornton dream of carving out an empire on the Texas frontier. The young couple is unprepared for just how much the dream will cost in this harsh land. Where will Daniel and Mary Anna find the strength to raise a family and make a home? Titles by author Linda Herring include: *Dreams of the Pioneers*, *Dreams of Glory*, *Dreams Fulfilled*, and *Song of Captivity*.

Historical, paperback, 464 pages, 5³/₁₆" x 8"

Heartsong

HEARTSONG PRESENTS TITLES AVAILABLE NOW:

__HP344 *The Measure of a Man*, C. Cox	__HP456 *The Cattle Baron's Bride*, C. Coble
__HP351 *Courtin' Patience*, K. Comeaux	__HP459 *Remnant of Light*, T. James
__HP352 *After the Flowers Fade*, A. Rognlie	__HP460 *Sweet Spring*, M. H. Flinkman
__HP356 *Texas Lady*, D. W. Smith	__HP463 *Crane's Bride*, L. Ford
__HP363 *Rebellious Heart*, R. Druten	__HP464 *The Train Stops Here*, G. Sattler
__HP371 *Storm*, D. L. Christner	__HP467 *Hidden Treasures*, J. Odell
__HP372 *'Til We Meet Again*, P. Griffin	__HP468 *Tarah's Lessons*, T. V. Bateman
__HP380 *Neither Bond Nor Free*, N. C. Pykare	__HP471 *One Man's Honor*, L. A. Coleman
__HP384 *Texas Angel*, D. W. Smith	__HP472 *The Sheriff and the Outlaw*, K. Comeaux
__HP387 *Grant Me Mercy*, J. Stengl	
__HP388 *Lessons in Love*, N. Lavo	__HP475 *Bittersweet Bride*, D. Hunter
__HP392 *Healing Sarah's Heart*, T. Shuttlesworth	__HP476 *Hold on My Heart*, J. A. Grote
	__HP479 *Cross My Heart*, C. Cox
__HP395 *To Love a Stranger*, C. Coble	__HP480 *Sonoran Star*, N. J. Farrier
__HP400 *Susannah's Secret*, K. Comeaux	__HP483 *Forever Is Not Long Enough*, B. Youree
__HP403 *The Best Laid Plans*, C. M. Parker	
__HP407 *Sleigh Bells*, J. M. Miller	__HP484 *The Heart Knows*, E. Bonner
__HP408 *Destinations*, T. H. Murray	__HP488 *Sonoran Sweetheart*, N. J. Farrier
__HP411 *Spirit of the Eagle*, G. Fields	__HP491 *An Unexpected Surprise*, R. Dow
__HP412 *To See His Way*, K. Paul	__HP492 *The Other Brother*, L. N. Dooley
__HP415 *Sonoran Sunrise*, N. J. Farrier	__HP495 *With Healing in His Wings*, S. Krueger
__HP416 *Both Sides of the Easel*, B. Youree	
__HP419 *Captive Heart*, D. Mindrup	__HP496 *Meet Me with a Promise*, J. A. Grote
__HP420 *In the Secret Place*, P. Griffin	__HP499 *Her Name Was Rebekah*, B. K. Graham
__HP423 *Remnant of Forgiveness*, S. Laity	
__HP424 *Darling Cassidy*, T. V. Bateman	__HP500 *Great Southland Gold*, M. Hawkins
__HP427 *Remnant of Grace*, S. K. Downs	__HP503 *Sonoran Secret*, N. J. Farrier
__HP428 *An Unmasked Heart*, A. Boeshaar	__HP504 *Mail-Order Husband*, D. Mills
__HP431 *Myles from Anywhere*, J. Stengl	__HP507 *Trunk of Surprises*, D. Hunt
__HP432 *Tears in a Bottle*, G. Fields	__HP508 *Dark Side of the Sun*, R. Druten
__HP435 *Circle of Vengeance*, M. J. Conner	__HP511 *To Walk in Sunshine*, S. Laity
__HP436 *Marty's Ride*, M. Davis	__HP512 *Precious Burdens*, C. M. Hake
__HP439 *One With the Wind*, K. Stevens	__HP515 *Love Almost Lost*, I. B. Brand
__HP440 *The Stranger's Kiss*, Y. Lehman	__HP516 *Lucy's Quilt*, J. Livingston
__HP443 *Lizzy's Hope*, L. A. Coleman	__HP519 *Red River Bride*, C. Coble
__HP444 *The Prodigal's Welcome*, K. Billerbeck	__HP520 *The Flame Within*, P. Griffin
__HP447 *Viking Pride*, D. Mindrup	__HP523 *Raining Fire*, L. A. Coleman
__HP448 *Chastity's Angel*, L. Ford	__HP524 *Laney's Kiss*, T. V. Bateman
__HP451 *Southern Treasures*, L. A. Coleman	__HP531 *Lizzie*, L. Ford
__HP452 *Season of Hope*, C. Cox	__HP532 *A Promise Made*, J. L. Barton
__HP455 *My Beloved Waits*, P. Darty	__HP535 *Viking Honor*, D. Mindrup

(If ordering from this page, please remember to include it with the order form.)

Presents

Great Inspirational Romance at a Great Price!

Heartsong Presents books are inspirational romances in
contemporary and historical settings, designed to give you an
enjoyable, spirit-lifting reading experience. You can choose
wonderfully written titles from some of today's best authors like
Peggy Darty, Sally Laity, DiAnn Mills, Colleen L. Reece,
Debra White Smith, and many others.

*When ordering quantities less than twelve, above titles are $2.97 each.
Not all titles may be available at time of order.*

SEND TO: **Heartsong Presents** Reader's Service
P.O. Box 721, Uhrichsville, Ohio 44683

Please send me the items checked above. I am enclosing $ _____
(please add $2.00 to cover postage per order. OH add 7% tax. NJ
add 6%). Send check or money order, no cash or C.O.D.s, please.

To place a credit card order, call 1-740-922-7280.

NAME _____

ADDRESS _____

CITY/STATE _____ ZIP_____

HPS 9-05